A DRUG
CALLED HORSE

A DRUG
CALLED
HORSE

Terry Waters

WOLFHOUND PRESS

First published 1990 by
WOLFHOUND PRESS,
68 Mountjoy Square,
Dublin 1.

Wolfhound Press receives financial assistance from
The Arts Council (An Chomhairle Ealaíon), Dublin, Ireland.

British Library Cataloguing in Publication Data
Waters, Terence
  A drug called horse.
  I. Title
  823'.914 [F]

ISBN 0-86327-258-4

5 4 3 2 1

Cover design: Jan de Fouw
Typesetting: Redsetter Ltd., Dublin.
Printed by The Guernsey Book Co., Guernsey.

A DRUG
CALLED HORSE

Chapter 1

'Au Revoir!'

The screw smirked, then closed the prison gate behind Tom Reid. Tom stood a while, face raised, soaking the heat of the early summer sun, the icy composure he'd carefully maintained this last year beginning to melt slowly in that first blissful moment of freedom. Eyes closed, his ears attuned themselves to the sounds of the outside world. The steady murmur of traffic was mocked occasionally by the raunchy screams of the seagulls. The echoes emanating from Mountjoy prison behind him reminded him to move. He began a dogtrot down the avenue between the parked Escorts and Kadetts of the prison guards, two hundred yards, the longest distance he'd covered in a straight line in a year. The murmur of traffic grew to a rumble as he neared the North Circular Road. His ears identified the component sounds, cars, trucks, people, and yes, horses. One or two. He looked. Against the everchanging background of traffic two seemingly unmoving animals. A hairy piebald with a rider aboard, the other a brown pony, part Connemara, part hunter. Yes, his horses. His and Joe's.

The man on the piebald was his brother Joe. Blond hair falling past his shoulders, smiling down at him. They wrung hands.

'Brother Joe,' he said simply in greeting.

'Your Christian Brother,' Joe laughed freely as Tom hadn't heard laughter in a year. Tom moved around the horses caressing them with all his body like a cat, purring the comforting sounds, appreciating their shining, bright-eyed health, nodding. Joe handed him the reins and he swung easily up on the bare back of the brown, gentling the animal easy with his knees. Joe handed him his tobacco and he rolled the first cigarette of many months.

Tom kneed the brown around and started up the North Circular Road. Joe wheeled in beside him riding at a walk along the pavement. A hundred yards later, due to the pedestrians, they were forced to dismount and lead the animals single file along the kerb. The two brothers continued so until they negotiated the two junctions and then re-mounted on the pavement and travelled along the Circular Road towards the Phoenix Park.

As they moved slowly through the red-bricked canyon past the site of the old cattle market, Tom grew more and more excited, anticipating the expanse of the Park. He and the pony were champing on the bit. As they entered the Park, Joe, sensing Tom's eagerness, said 'Wait for me at the Islandbridge Gate'.

They cantered until they reached the edge of the Fifteen Acres, where a bloodcurdling yell erupted from Tom as he took off at a gallop, the anarchist's flag of his long black hair flowing behind him. Joe watched him fly, cantering along behind, his workaday mare out for a leisurely outing in the park. Tom on the spirited brown, his racer, was free at last.

Chapter 2

Tom 'Tonto' Reid – Tonto, because physically he looked a picturegoers idea of an Indian. His coal-black hair fell below his shoulder-blades, his nose, due to a hurling accident was hooked, aquiline. His ruddy outdoor complexion and his bearing was warrior-like. He did, besides, possess an aboriginal stoicism, an uncanny affinity with animals and an innate savagery, terrible when released. He had but one brother, Joe, and a mother and father in their late sixties, who were very much alive. His family was unusually small, his parents having children at an age when their contemporaries were becoming grandparents. His mother was a small sturdy dark woman, an intensely political Liberties girl of the revolution, the Civil war and the Black and Tans. Her heroes were Larkin and Connolly. The father was a Connemara man who, though fifty years out of it, still thought in Irish. Rose and Martin, after twenty years in pagan England, ended up in a brand new Ballyfermot in the Fifties. Their first son Tom was born into a home full of argument, radical politics, and the hazy mysticism of the Atlantic seaboard. Joe soon followed and the family was complete.

Ballyfermot then was the edge of the city. Its nearest neighbours were the villages of Bluebell, Fox and Geese, Clondalkin, Lucan and Chapelizod, sandwiched between open farmland, the canal on one side and the Liffey on the other. Children by the thousand poured into this vast adventure playground. Room here for every child's fantasy. Materials aplenty for the manufacture of the essential playthings and tools of boyhood – the bow and arrow, the sling, the spear, the tomahawk, the chestnut for conkers. From the manufacture of these they learned the practical skills of the hands. In the canal they taught themselves to swim; in the Liffey, to fish. A wonderful education of the body, mind and soul, interrupted unfortunately by the woeful obligation to attend school. Into this paradise annually came that nomadic tribe, the travellers. They appeared with their horses, dogs, wagons and their music. Adults, families with children who lived in tents, cooked their meals on campfires, just like the Indians, and who didn't have to go home to a house at night. Tom was drawn immediately as if to a magnet, and as always Joe followed. Within days he was on a pony, his fate was sealed. He was five, Joe was three. By the time he was seven he had a pony of his own. At eight he went for the first time with one of the travelling families on the road. When he returned for school he was deeply tanned, his geography was the best in his class, and he had traded the pony for a good piebald mare in foal. Through his father's friendship with a man called Jobber Whelan, who kept a small farm locally, Tom acquired grazing and a life-long friend.

At eleven he had two piebald mares, one good pony and a foal, and a cart on the road selling logs and moving furniture. That's when he quit school. Two years later Joe joined him full-time. That year, through an astute piece of trading, they acquired a brood mare of exceptional breeding. Almost a thoroughbred, from an Arab dam and a Cob sire. It cost them three of their best animals. They now had the mother of a superb herd. His original mentor, the patriarch of the Small family, Walter, seeing her, offered to take the mare and have her covered.

'I know the perfect sire,' he said 'but I'll have to take her to West Cork. At our rate of travel you'll not see her again for some time. You'll have to give her into my hands and trust me.'

Tom agreed readily. He was fifteen by the time the mare returned, accompanied by the most beautiful chestnut stallion colt he had ever seen. He had the father of his herd. 'The sire is a thoroughbred hunter,' Walter explained, 'but I've no papers I'm afraid, as the owner, God bless his gentlemanly heart, would not have approved of the coupling had he known.'

Tom Reid at fifteen had achieved what most men never

achieve in a lifetime – his dream.

That same year Tom courted a young girl, Marie Cummins. Wise as he was in the world of horse-trading, this was an area in which he was totally naïve. They were just two children who lost themselves in marathon kisses and silly argument. Her father, a clerk with C.I.E., did not approve of this 'knacker'. His disapproval only succeeded in making Tom more attractive in the eyes of the impressionable Marie. Rebellion took the form of a fumbling and totally unsatisfying intercourse. She became pregnant. Tom could see no alternative but marriage, and Marie glowed in anticipation. Her father however could not accept that Tom had a job and forbade the marriage. The couple in their frustration and immaturity turned this small wrinkle into a major issue and refused to talk to each other.

A son was born to Marie, and remarkably was christened Thomas. Rose, on the birth of her grandson, with her usual impatience with what she called 'bullshite', simply collected the boy as often as she felt was her granny's right. Thus, Tom saw his son as much as, if not more than, many of the legitimate young fathers around. Young Tommy was on horseback as young as his father was before him, and at six had a pony of his own.

Successful as their parenthood may have been, the frustration between the couple continued and they grew further apart with the years.

Chapter 3

At the age of twenty-five Tom was sentenced to a year in prison, convicted of inflicting grievous bodily harm.

They'd had a pony stolen – not an unusual event in these strange times. After a period of perhaps ten years of unprecedented prosperity, mass unemployment had returned to the city. Relative poverty bred great dissatisfaction among the huge young population. The older people quickly resigned themselves to the return of an adversary they had fought many times. They had the weapons of familiarity. The young, however, had never developed the antibodies to resist this social disease.

In their hopelessness they turned to the antibiotics society now offered – the old placebo alcohol, the new placeboes, hash and glue. The truly disenchanted turned to the most deadly anaesthetic of all, heroin. Sometimes teenagers sought the escape of their childhood fantasies. Galloping on a pony they were again as hopeful as children, riding the endless prairies of their imaginations. Generally they treated the animals well enough, drove them a little hard perhaps, but usually returned them close to where they'd taken them from. If caught, they accepted the punishment and that was generally that.

Leaving Joe to take care of business, Tom began the arduous task of retrieving the pony. Finally, following a reliable report, he entered 'the backers'.

'The backers' was an area of farmland acquired for development during the good years. Due to the recession the land lay unused. Over the years it had reverted back to nature. It was wild country, surrounded on three sides by 'Ballyer', Cold Cut and Clondalkin, and on the fourth side by the long narrow valley of the railway line west.

An area inhabited by the runaways of the surrounding suburbs, it was frequented only by the hunters and trappers of the area, men with ferrets, dogs and snares. Rabbits were killed and wild birds trapped for sale in the bird markets. The lack of roads and density of brush rendered it inaccessible to police patrols. It was outlaw country. The formidable task of finding the pony in this semi-jungle annoyed Tom, but the task proved a lot easier than he'd anticipated. He heard the agonised whinnies of the animal from a distance. He ran towards the sound. At the scene he was stopped momentarily by the horror of what he saw. Five crazed teenagers were dragging the screaming pony through a blazing bonfire. Tom's hold on his monumental temper slipped. He went berserk. Five broken teenagers and a dead pony remained when dazed he left the scene.

In court, the judge summed up: 'However well-intentioned and justified this young man's actions may have been, the brute savagery of his assaults leaves the court no alternative but to sentence him to one year's imprisonment. People must be made to fully understand the seriousness of taking the law into their own hands.'

Chapter 4

A year later Tom sat on a hill in the Phoenix Park waiting for his brother to catch up. He watched the silver sweep of the Liffey below him. Joe cantered into view.

Leaving his mount to the luxury of the sweet grass Joe sat by his brother. 'Took your time,' Tom joked.

Joe rolled a cigarette and passed the tobacco.

They smoked in silence, listening to the munching of the contented animals. When they finished their smokes Joe mounted and walked the mare down the hill towards the Park gate. When Tom caught up Joe explained, 'I'm bringing you this way to show you something.'

Tom had wondered why they had not continued through the Park to the Chapelizod gate, a far more pleasant ride.

They led the horses across the busy western road, over the bridge to the entrance of the Memorial Park. Here they remounted and trotted along by the river. Slowing to a walk they ascended the hill, skirting the First World War Memorial. From the height Tom saw immediately what Joe had wanted him to see.

What a year ago had been a hundred acres of rough, but serviceable grazing, was now a moonscape of naked brown earth. A long artificially flat-bottomed valley swerved through the mountains of disturbed clay and boulders.

'A sign of the times brother, a new motorway,' Joe explained sadly.

'Jesus!' Tom exclaimed, 'where are the lads keeping their stocks now?'

Only one year ago, over fifty horses had been grazed here.

Now back home, Tom's mother ladled out a large bowl of her delicious stew, and placed it beside a plate piled with heavily-buttered fresh turnover. Tom ate hungrily. Carefully she poured a bottle of Guinness into a glass, setting the head just right. She placed it before her eldest son, and silently watched him eat. He finished the bowl and she quickly refilled it. He finished the second bowl and all of the bread.

Finally, she spoke, voicing the most harmless of the thousand questions she longed to ask. 'They feed you at all?'

'Sure,' Tom replied, 'but not like this.'

'We expected you home three months ago.' It was a question.

'I was turned down for parole.' Seeing the further question on her face, he continued, 'I found it necessary to assert myself a few times. I was not an ideal prisoner.'

She grinned at the understatement, but her sadness prevailed. 'Jesus, Tom, I feel so damned guilty sometimes. Martin and I were so old having you, so set in our ways, so sure. As the eldest you got it all. It's more than just for health reasons we should have our children while we're young. It's for being innocent and unsure and learning together. We'd been together so long fighting the bullshite, we'd long since lost patience with it. But you, you just inherited the impatience without the forty years of getting there.' She stopped, staring out the window. Tom stood, taking her by the shoulders, turned her to face him. 'Look at me,' he said softly, 'and listen. I came out of there this morning the same man who went in. I'm not bitter or angry, and my pride is intact. If I fought, I fought only for that right, the right to come out as I went in. If it cost me three months, it was worth it. I saw men in there lose their pride, be made small. It's like the whole system is geared to that. Not just the screws, the prisoners themselves. If they can make you feel small, they can think themselves bigger. That impatience you worry about is not wrong. It's so damned right. We have to be impatient with bullshite. Otherwise we might just accept it. Ma, I wasn't innocent going in there, but I sure as be Jaysus didn't feel guilty. The last thing I want to hear in the world is that you feel guilty. Stop it, Ma. It doesn't suit you. Now did you forget something?'

'What?' she asked seriously.

'My dessert,' he laughed.

'I have not,' she said, 'I made rhubarb tart and custard.'

'Well you better get it on the table, because I'm still hungry.'

As Tom ate the dessert his mother made a pot of tea. She was pouring when a voice spoke from the door. 'Tea. I'd a thought whiskey more appropriate for an occasion like this.'

A tall grizzled man stood in the doorway smiling savagely. Salt and pepper hair hung over eyes that seemed to hold all the hues of the sea.

'Martin!'

The blow to the chest Tom received on approaching told him his father had lost none of his strength nor his speed. 'The Connemara handshake.'

They hugged like two bears, affectionately testing each other. Satisfied, they parted and laughed their pleasure at seeing each other again.

Joe had poured four generous glasses of whiskey. The toast was 'Welcome home Tom'.

Chapter 5

The brothers arose early next morning. Tom's hangover was monumental, his system reacting badly to the unaccustomed intake of alcohol. Noting Joe's serene composure he wondered if his young brother ever felt extreme about anything.

'Not enough practice,' Joe remarked, reading Tom's mind. 'To be a good drinker you have to practice every day.'

'Anything on today?' Tom asked.

'I was going up to the Jobbers to get one of the other mares. We've a few jobs on the next couple of days. We'll need both carts working.'

'Great,' Tom said, 'I'm dying to see the stallion and the new foals. The walk will do me good.'

They led the brown pony into a warm summer's morning. The streets were alive with kids squeezing every possible moment from their precious time away from school.

'Give us a ride on your horse, Mister?'

When they reached the 'Lawns' they sat awhile smoking, allowing the Brown to graze. Tom was beginning to feel a little better. The manicured expanse of the 'Lawns' bristled with good weather activity. Young mothers sat in groups talking, playing youths kicked ball, their shouts ringing in the morning quiet, unemployed men lay in circles playing endless games of Don, each game followed by the more pleasurable argument of the Post Mortem. Tom absorbed it greedily. It was all new again.

Not wanting the pony to devour too much grass, they reluctantly moved on. Cherry Orchard hospital gleamed in the sunshine, the Cypress trees still in the breathless air.

Opposite, an industrial estate covered the site of the travellers encampment where twenty years before the brothers had been initiated into the world of horses. Here, for many years, the biggest winter stopping place in the country had prospered. That cross-roads field had seen the birth and death of many travellers. The smokey air filled with the music of accordeon and fiddle, of argument and laughter. Here they had learned the giddy pleasure of freedom.

The road they took now was narrow, an old country road, wide enough for two trucks, but now serving the new housing estates that surrounded Clondalkin. The constant stream of impatient motorists made it very difficult for pedestrians, more so leading a nervous pony. Traffic had to stop and wait to go round them. Reaching the Jobber's gate was a great relief. The old man himself was leaning over the gate and greeted them with obvious pleasure. He merely smiled at Joe, but grabbed Tom by the shoulders. 'Let me look at yeh,' he demanded. 'By God they didn't change yeh. You look just fine Tom, just fine. Here, give me that pony. I'll put him out, ye go on into the house.'

The house was a single storey cottage. Never having married, the Jobber kept the house as his grandfather had built it. A wife would have wanted a bungalow like the neighbours. He was extremely comfortable in his little house. All but two of his neighbours had sold out to developers. This was very valuable real estate. Those remaining valued their homes of many generations more than the fabulous sums of money offered.

At eighty-one, the Jobber did very little farming now. He grew some spuds and onions in a small garden and allowed the brothers to use his fields and buildings for their horses. He took an interest in their efforts and great delight in their successes.

Inside the house Joe wet tea. A black kettle on the range held a constant supply of hot water. Two dogs lay on the stone floor, occasionally flicking their tails, stirring the fine ash dust that hovered constantly in the air. On his return the Jobber said to Joe: 'You know where the whiskey is. Sweeten the tea. Tom looks a wee bit shaky.'

The three sat quietly for a while, hearing only the sounds of the birds, the occasional whinny of the horses and the swishing of the dogs' tails. The Jobber began the slow, careful ritual of filling his pipe. They might have been in the heart of the country instead of where they were, surrounded on all sides by a million people.

The old man began to speak. 'I'm as isolated here as if I were at the end of a mountain boreen in furthest County Kerry. Since the traffic increased on that road out there I haven't had a caller. Nobody walks that road anymore. Before, on a Sunday afternoon I could lean on my gate and talk to twenty or thirty people. When the blackberry season came I was pestered here with kids. Not even a beggar now to pass an evening with. If it wasn't for you two boys and your Da now and then I wouldn't see a soul from one week to the next that wasn't sitting in a car.'

He lapsed into silence, seeming to doze off. Joe poured more tea.

The old man spoke again. 'When are your mates bringing the stallion back?'

The two brothers looked at each other.

'What's that, Jobber?' Joe enquired.

'Those lads who collected the stud yesterday, to cover the mare. Said you were too busy to be there yourself.' He hesitated, the realisation penetrating. 'Ye didn't know.' The old man felt sick.

Joe shook his head. The three rose and made for the paddock. Perhaps the old man was dreaming. The stallion was gone. Tom's mind spun. His prize stallion. His proudest achievement. His herd only now, after so many years, starting to reflect the quality of its original sire. The brown racer, his brood mares and the two excellent horses standing before him now. After the shock, the anger grew. Uncontrolled, it had cost him a year of his life, but he could taste it, like concussion.

The Jobber crossed himself.

Joe hurriedly rolled and lit a cigarette, and passed it to Tom, who drew on it, taking smoke down deep into his lungs, and held it until his eyes watered, then exhaled with a deep exaggerated sigh. Five times he repeated this exercise, making himself calm.

Joe finally spoke. 'Alright?'

The answer was a bitter 'Yeah'.

Joe addressed the Jobber. 'Will you make tea, Jobber, while we check the rest. We'll be in in a minute.'

He turned to Tom and said firmly, 'Get in and check the foals.' It was calculated on Joe's part, this request. He knew Tom better than anybody else. He knew that for Tom to enter that field, to touch those animals he would have to be completely calm. To mingle among them in anger would be a grievous sin to Tom. It would alienate him from the animals, perhaps breach irreparably the oneness with them that was all-important to him. Sometimes he felt this was the reason horses meant so very much to his brother. They were his sanity, where he found his self balance.

Joe whispered 'Go on, Tom, go on.'

Tom went among the herd, moving quietly from one to the next, touching and gently murmuring. With the foals, who shyly trembled, unused to him, he was gentleness itself. Rejoining Joe at the fence, he accepted another cigarette and began to formulate his thoughts. They returned to the house.

The Jobber sat fretting, sipping a large glass of whiskey.

'Boys,' he almost cried, 'Jesus I'm so sorry.'

Tom sat by him, placing his arm around the old man's shoulder. 'Hey now,' as if speaking to a child, 'it's not your fault. You couldn't know.'

'I should have,' Jobber interrupted. 'They were too well dressed, and what they knew about handling horses was sweet fuck all.'

'Relax now, fill your pipe and then tell us exactly what happened.'

While he did this the brothers poured tea and made themselves cigarettes.

Chapter 6

The old man began his story. 'They came about half eleven yesterday morning. They had the whole road blocked out there trying to get that trailer in backwards. A few times they tried before they got it right. It made my morning, laughing at the antics of them, cursing at each other. They were two good-humoured lads, big, tough-looking boys. They said Joe told them he was meeting you, and what a shame it was you getting nicked like that. They explained their mare was in heat and you said it was okay for them to take the stud themselves. There was more crack when they were trying to get the stallion into the trailer. No hurry on them either. We had tea and a chat. When they were leaving they gave me a tenner for a drink, they said, then drove off laughing and waving. Said they'd drop in if ever they were passing.'

Tom asked what kind of car they were driving.

'A blue Mercedes, looked new.'

There was silence for a while as the information sank in.

'A few things strike me,' Tom remarked. 'They came at the exact moment Joe was meeting me. They could have taken the stallion any time, but waited for that particular moment. Another thing, that stallion may be invaluable to us, but Arkle he is not. A new Mercedes would buy ten of him.'

Joe spoke, 'It looks like someone is out to hurt you, Tom. I mean I've no enemies. I presume that everybody in the Joy wasn't your friend.'

'Sure, I made enemies,' Tom agreed, 'but that was in the beginning. Once I convinced them all I wanted was to be left alone, that was that. The ones I actually hurt were just hired muscle. It was just part of the job for them. The ones in a position to set up a thing like this wouldn't bother. They were content to know that I wasn't trying to cut in on their action. No, Joe, it's not from prison. It just doesn't sit right.'

The Jobber spoke. 'It strikes me, the lads who came weren't the slightest bit nervous, like stealing a horse was nothing to them. It was a day out in the country for them.'

'So they were pros,' Joe spoke now. 'It looks like what it cost to steal the stallion would have bought one as good.'

'We can keep talking about this all day,' Tom concluded. 'Someone is out to get me, that's for sure. The only way to find out who it is, is to wait or find the stallion. We're stuck with the waiting, so let's look. Seeing as the stallion could be anywhere in the country we need help, a lot of help.'

Tom turned to Jobber. 'Old friend,' he said quietly, 'don't worry about this. It's no fault of yours. Whoever is behind this was determined it would succeed, so no matter what, they would have done it. We'd never have been able to forgive ourselves if you'd been hurt. We owe everything we have to you, and believe me we're grateful, Joe and me. We'll sort this out – okay?'

'You boys are the only family I've got,' the Jobber said. 'Every success you've had has been my success. But Tom, listen to an old man, keep hold of that temper of yours. It's a gift of God's as well as the devil's, so use it well. Be careful, lads.'

Chapter 7

They took leave of their old friend. At the road they stopped and Joe asked: 'What now?'

'We need the help of people who nose around the whole country, and luckily we know such people,' Tom answered.

'The travellers?'

'Right.'

The nearest encampment was just beyond the new prison. They made their way there. About twenty prefab buildings of simple design, on littered ground. Parked outside of each dwelling a vehicle. Over all hung an atmosphere of impermanence as if the spectre of the uncompleted prison predisposed its desertion. A teenage boy met them immediately they entered the gate.

'Who d'ya want?' he demanded.

'Charlie Cash,' Tom told him.

'And your business?'

'With him!' Tom was purposely sharp.

The boy sauntered off and was gone awhile. He re-appeared and beckoned. They followed. A group of men stood sullenly around a fire. Recognising Tom, the eldest man came forward, smiling, his hand outstretched.

'Tonto Reid!' he exclaimed. 'We thought you were still in prison.'

'Got out yesterday,' Tom replied. 'How are you Charlie?'

'Grand, grand, except for that,' he complained, nodding in the direction of the prison wall. 'You couldn't live in the shadow of that.'

'I can understand that,' Tom quipped.

'Indeed you can, indeed you can,' Charlie said, laughing. 'I'd have thought you'd be celebrating somewhere, not visiting this unlucky place.'

'I need your help, Charlie,' Tom explained, and told him what had happened.

'Aye, you've an enemy there, Tom,' he agreed. He addressed the other men and they departed, each driving off in a different vehicle.

'They'll start the word going. Ye're walking?' he asked. Tom nodded in reply.

'We best see the old man, I'll drive you over to Labre.'

Charlie's car proved to be a new Volvo, so they travelled in style to Labre Park. Unlike the place by the prison, Labre Park was neat, the area around the prefabs clear of scrap, in front of each dwelling a small cultivated garden. They entered one of the chalets. Seated at a table was a white-haired, bearded old man.

Walter Small, uncrowned king of the travellers, Tom's old mentor, his travelling grandfather.

'Grandfather,' Tom greeted him formally, shaking his hand.

'My son,' Walter observed the same formality. Turning to Joe he greeted him likewise.

'I had hoped to visit you in better circumstances,' Tom apologised.

'I am pleased to see you, and glad you think of me in time of need. You have guessed your story preceded you. Already my instructions are given. My people will be your eyes and ears. Your stallion will be found, have no fear.'

Walter lived with his daughter, a widow, who'd returned to his house when her own family had grown. She shyly laid the table now, the best china. She poured tea for the men, then left the house.

The old man, nearly ninety, Tom guessed, still retained all his wily intelligence.

'It is a heavy blow for you, Tom, this thing. You for whom prison must have been especially painful. You who cherish freedom so much more than most house-dwellers. I say this as your grandfather, Tom. You have not the forbearance of your brother. Your anger, your pain must be great. I ask you to put this matter aside, leave it in our hands, for there is nothing you can do until the stallion is located. Put it from your mind for now. Enjoy your freedom, get drunk, take a woman. Go

among your horses. You have young animals to train. Do these
things and leave the rest to me.'

Tom thought for a while. 'There's damn all else I can do,' he
agreed. 'Your advice is sound. I'll give it a go.'

They talked awhile more before leaving. Joe accepted a lift
from Charlie. He still had to collect a mare from the Jobbers.
Tom decided it was time to see his son. He took the longer
route along the canal. The time alone he used to prepare
himself for the difficult task ahead. This was going to be as
hard as being imprisoned. Well, he'd survived that. He'd be
damned if he couldn't handle a little waiting. He walked the
distance between the sixth and seventh locks without meeting
a soul. At the bridge he sat and watched the kids swimming.
Seeing the pleasure they were having jumping and diving off
the lock, and the manic dogpaddle of the novice swimmers,
drove his problem from his mind. He searched the faces of the
boys, wondering if his son was among them. He was not. The
house where Marie now lived was a mile from the canal. He
was there in twenty minutes. She sat in the front garden with
another young woman. An infant lay on a blanket between
them.

'Hello Marie.' He smiled at her and the other woman.

'The young fellow was waiting for you last night,' she
snapped in reply. 'This is Angela.' She introduced her friend.

'Howya Angela,' he answered. 'If I'm not mistaken I went to
school with your brother Brian.'

'That's right. He's in London now,' Angela said. 'I'll tell him
I met you in the next letter.'

'How are you?' Marie enquired.

'Grand,' he replied and asked 'Where's Tommy now?'

'He's on the Lawns playing football,' she told him.

'I'll go find him so.' Tom prepared to leave.

'Come back with him, Tom,' Marie said, adding, '– for tea.
I'd like to talk to you.'

'Okay,' Tom said, 'I'll see you later so. Bye.'

On the Lawns there were several games of soccer going on,
so it took Tom some time to find the boy. He was deeply
involved in a five-a-side. It was a fast, furious game, so Tom
lay on the grass and watched. Not having seen the boy play
before, he became very interested and impressed by what he

saw. The boy, while not the best footballer on the field, displayed a fair skill, coupled with courage and enthusiasm aligned with good humour. He was a credit to the team. Tom experienced a pride in his son he had never felt before. He was saddened to think of the year he had lost of the boy's growing up, as indeed the boy had grown up a great deal in that year.

The match finished and Tom saw one of his son's teammates pointing in his direction. Tommy ran to him and jumped into his arms.

'Da! Da!' he exclaimed. 'Howya?'

'Great. You played well. Did ye win?'

'Yeah,' he said proudly, 'we milled them.'

Tommy waved at his friends as they left. Shyly, the boy explained 'You're kind of a hero, the way it was in the papers and all. They think you shouldn't have been sent to jail.'

'Do you think the same?'

'Yea, course.'

'Your Ma told me to bring you home for your tea. You must be starved.'

'She was raging you didn't come last night.'

'Jesus, she told me you were.'

'No, I knew you wouldn't. I was expecting you today.'

'Listen,' Tom said, 'don't tell her you told me that. She'll only be more raging.'

Father and son strolled together across the Lawns towards the shop. The boy chattered happily. They bought cans of Coke and drank them as they walked towards the house.

'You know there is a race on in the Park Sunday week?' the boy asked excitedly. 'Joe reckons I'm ready to enter in the pony race this time. Can I?'

'Well, if Joe says so, it must be so. It's fine with me. What about Marie?'

'You'll talk to her, won't you?' Tommy suggested confidently.

'Will she listen to me, though?' Tom asked.

At the house Marie had the table laid. She told Tommy to go and wash, and spoke to Tom. 'First thing I want to say is that I'm really sorry about you going to jail. I don't think it was right. You didn't deserve it. But unfortunately it has made you a hero with Tommy and his mates. I can't stop Tommy wanting to be with you, you are his father, and a good father, but I have plans for him. I want him to get a proper education. I want him to go to College. I hope you'll help me in this. The good thing about his interest in horses is that he'd like to be a vet. Will you encourage him?'

'Jesus, Marie,' Tom said, 'of course I will. I'm not trying to make him a little me. I turned him onto horses because it gives him a sense of responsibility. It's a useful interest. I watched him play football today and he made me very proud. He puts his heart into what he does. He shows courage and good humour and intelligence. And a vet, that would be great.'

'That's good, Tom,' Marie said with relief.

'There's one thing,' Tom said, 'Tommy wants to race on Sunday week. Joe thinks he's ready, and I believe the competition would be good for him. Will you let him?'

'He is growing up, I can't keep protecting him. Why not?'

During the tea Tom buried his feelings about the missing stallion and enjoyed the cheerful company of Marie and their son.

Chapter 8

With the advice of Walter Small foremost in his mind Tom threw himself wholeheartedly into his work. He breakfasted well each morning and spent two hours chopping logs. If any deliveries needed doing he harnessed one of the mares to a cart and did these before lunch. Afternoons, when free, he spent at the Jobbers. Here he began the training of two young ponies. Tommy usually joined him for these training sessions. This aspect of animal handling Tom felt was an essential part of the boy's apprenticeship, demanding as it did, great patience and discipline. They usually had tea with the Jobber, then began the part Tommy enjoyed most, preparing both their mounts for the up-and-coming race meeting. Every evening they exercised Tommy's pony and Tom's brown, both progeny of the missing stallion. Tom had won six races already with the brown. Joe had ridden him to victory twice in Tom's absence. Joe joined them most days. He and the Jobber, however, spent most of their time refurbishing an old trap that Joe had acquired. Both had considerable carpentry skill but it was the fact that Jobber had grown up in the time when the trap was the everyday transport that made his contribution so valuable. They hoped to have it ready for the races. The old man was thrilled that he might be able to drive his friends, Martin and Rose, to watch their sons and grandson racing.

In the evenings the tired trio walked back to Ballyfermot. Tommy was left home to Marie. Sometimes they ate there but mostly the brothers ate at their mother's house. Their father was seldom home as he and a friend were renovating an old cottage in Wicklow and usually stayed there.

After dinner Tom and Joe went together to the pub. Both were both card players, so they usually passed the time playing Solo. Joe's girlfriend came before closing time most nights and he'd go home with her. On the fourth night after his release Tom decided it was time to heed the first part of Walter's advice. Instead of going to the local, he dressed up and went into town. It was three days before he returned home. The following day he resumed his usual routine. Tommy was the only one who questioned his absence. Tom explained that he'd been on a bit of a tear.

The race being only five days away, both brothers spent more time coaching the boy. The trap was now ready, so the Jobber began repairing the old harness, his ancient hands struggling with the task, but he refused all help at what he classified as an old art. 'An old fart at an old art,' he laughingly described himself. At the Jobber's instigation Tommy invited Marie to ride in the trap to the races. She accepted willingly and immediately went shopping for an outfit. Joe observed: 'Think's she's going to Ascot.' Young Tommy responded: 'The mascot.'

Joe finally decided which of the mares he was going to ride in the hairy horse race and began exercising her in the evenings, much to the amusement of the others. While the pony galloped she burst into a plod.

Race meetings of the kind they were about to attend were held three or four times a year. They were organized by the various pony clubs throughout the city. These clubs were loose-knit organizations of people who made their living with horses and ponies. Most of the housing schemes boasted a club, each club electing a representative to a city council. The council selected a venue for the meeting and picked a date.

The Phoenix Park was the usual venue, being central to the whole city. As everybody concerned travelled there on horseback or by horse-drawn transport, distance had to be considered. Each meeting fielded three races – a hairy horse race, which was a novelty race for the heavy cart horses, a pony race for young riders, and a speed race for the better-bred horses. This last one was the prestige race. Winning this race multiplied the value of the animal concerned. Tom's missing stallion had produced three winners of the races so far, two of which he had sold. The brothers' reputation as the breeders of fine animals was countrywide due to their wins. These meetings were beginning to attract interested buyers from all over the country.

The day of the races finally dawned. Young Tommy was at the brothers' door at seven that morning. After breakfast, they accepted a lift from one of Tom's friends, and drove to the Jobber's. The morning was spent grooming all the animals involved. One of the breeding mares was selected to draw the trap. She was a pretty brown and she shone like a chestnut between the shafts. The Jobber, freshly shaved, donned his best suit and his real Stetson hat. Tom adapted his Tonto outfit – fringed buckskin shirt and moccasins, a red bandana tied around his head. Ready for the big parade. Trap in front of the riders in single file behind, they set off for Ballyfermot. Marie's was the first stop. She boarded the trap resplendent in red dress, red shoes and white picture hat, to the cheers of her neighbours. At the brothers' house, Martin, in a three-piece tweed suit, gallantly helped Rose onto the trap and lifted in the large picnic basket. The three riders wolf-whistled at Rose's mauve costume and black hat.

Here the riders and the trap separated, the riders to join the other horsemen at Lynch's Lane, the trap to join the other vehicles at the Lawns.

Before reaching the rendezvous the lads were joined by several others. They were nine in all by the time they reached Lynch's Lane. Here were thirty-seven more horses, all in flamboyant attire. There were horses and ponies, piebalds and skewbalds, blacks, whites and palominos. Animals, good, bad and indifferent. The riders, all bareback, ranged in age from eleven to fifty. Most favoured the wardrobe of the cowboy or the Indian. Despite the hot weather, ponchoes were the favourite garment. Hats were of every description. The Indians were more sensibly dressed for the weather – headbands, some with feathers, and sleeveless shirts or jackets. One fifty-year-old Teddy Boy rode resplendent in royal blue drapes, skin-tight black trousers and brothel-creepers, his hair shining in a brilliantined D.A.

Most dismounted and smoked, waiting for the horse-drawn

brigade to arrive and take the lead. Families began to gather along the footpath anticipating the parade. A parade was a rare event these days. The cheering of the crowd heralded the arrival of the horse-drawns, twenty-seven in all. Mostly the families of the riders, they were led by a four-wheeled coal wagon, polished clean, on the back of which played a five-piece band. Four-wheeled and two-wheeled carts, mostly home-made, working transport all. There were Sunday buggies of all descriptions, again mostly home-made.

The riders mounted and fell in behind, two- to three-abreast. A passing squad car not wanting to be left out took the lead with hazard lights flashing. The route chosen was the least steep hill into the valley of Chapelizod, down by the Memorial Park.

The cavalcade moved slowly. As they passed down the hill a contingent of travellers fell in behind. The squad car led until they reached the Park gate, where it pulled off to one side and officiously took up traffic duty, halting cars, while the parade entered the Park. In the Park the caravan passed up around Mary's Hospital and onto the plain that stretched out behind. Off in the distance could be seen the already-gathered crowd. As they approached, the stewards separated the riders from the rest, directing them towards the picket-line set up to accommodate their mounts. Ropes slung out along stakes driven solidly into the ground. The vehicles were led by the stewards to create two lines, fifty feet apart. This would be the track. Already it stretched over two hundred yards and more were yet to come. The atmosphere was that of a carnival and a horse fair.

With the animals tied up under the watchful eye of the men assigned to see to their welfare, Tom and Joe went looking for friends, Tommy looking for his own. Already the dealing had begun, animals and carts changing hands. The brothers examined a palomino mare that interested them, but decided to wait until later before broaching a deal. Their success in the racing, and more so in the betting, would determine their trading position. They joined a group from Finglas, one of whom had been in jail with Tom. They began drinking. It turned out that the theft of Tom's stallion was common knowledge, and Tom's prison friend agreed that it was unlikely the theft emanated from enemies made there. The brothers circulated. Tom was favourite in the big race. The best price he or Joe could get was even money. This did not prevent them from accepting any bets they were offered. They walked along the track until they found the trap. The Jobber and Martin had obviously started in on the poitín. Rose and Marie had gone strolling.

Martin observed: 'I can only get evens on you, Tom. What do you think?'

'It's not bad, Da, take what you can get,' Tom told him, 'there's nothing we can't beat.'

'What's young Tommy's chances?' Martin asked.

Joe answered. 'His pony is as good as anything he'll be up against. He's a grand rider. The only problem is lack of experience in the both of them.'

Martin produced a bottle, offering it to his sons. Both refused. They walked to the starting area to talk with the stewards, and to pay their entrance fees. The fee for the hairy horse race was five pounds, with perhaps forty entrants.

'That should be some crack,' the steward commented.

Tom paid the ten pounds for Tommy to go in the pony race, fifteen entrants. It cost him twenty to enter the big race, with a field of twelve. The prize money was made up of the entrance fee, divided in half for the winner, a third for second, and a sixth for third place. The main event was winner take all.

Joe went to prepare his mare for the first race. It would begin in fifteen minutes. Tom found Tommy and they made their way to the trap to watch the race in style.

The best the stewards could do at the starting line with the mass of heavy horses was to get them all facing in the right direction. The whistle blew. The race began with what looked like a battle. The horses, unused to this carry-on, were milling in every direction bar forward. Riders pulled from their mounts by other riders were scuttling away from the hooves of the massive animals. Nobody downed bothered to remount. Five horses, with riders, managed to pull free from the bunch and began plodding down the field. They were harrassed at all sides by the riderless mounts who were proving much faster than those with riders. Two riders moved clear. Joe was one, and a man from Cabra was the other. The race began. The course was four hundred yards in all.

They were more than half-way, and with much shouting and kicking they urged the animals towards the line. With turf flying they crossed the line. Joe was beaten by a head. It was half a minute before the third horse crossed. Joe collected sixty pounds. He was well pleased.

Tommy met him and took the mare to the picket line. Joe made his way to the trap, and this time accepted the drink from his father.

Gasping from the poitín, he said, 'I should be using this on the outside for my bruises.'

Martin laughed, 'You had me worried there for a while, I thought you were going to win. I'd a fiver on the other fella at six to one.'

The brothers went off to find Tommy. He was at the picket, surrounded by his mates, advice flying from every angle. Joe addressed him. 'First off, relax, there are fifteen ponies in your race, so don't think it'll be like the one I was in. There will be plenty of room to line up properly. Your pony is as fast as any of the others but he's not used to the crowds. So your big concern will be keeping him under control. The course is five hundred yards, so you give stick right from the start. Once you're going it's a speed race. Right?'

Tommy nodded.

'So,' Joe concluded, 'good luck.'

Marie and Tom walked the boy to the starting area. Tom shook his hand and nodded his wishes but much to his embarrassment Marie hugged him. He mounted and walked the pony to the line. Tom, to his surprise, found his arm around Marie's waist.

As Joe had said, he had plenty of space. He was near the centre of the line. The pony was very nervous, and it took all his time to keep him from bucking. The whistle blew, but the pony was uneasy and he was the last to leave the line. Seeing the rest go, he kicked the pony into motion. Once moving, the pony was grand and he began to catch the field. One by one he passed them, and with fifty yards to go he was second and gaining. At the line there was only a nose in it. Unfortunately, it was the other pony's. He felt like crying. If only.

Joe was at the finish line. 'You did great,' he yelled excitedly, 'the way you passed them all. Another yard and you'd have won. Jesus from so far back. Next time out nobody will beat you.'

'The start . . .' Tommy began.

'The next time you'll know,' Joe reassured him. 'That was a magic first time. That pony is faster than I thought. Come on, you'll feel better with a fistful of money.

And he did. With fifty pounds he was richer than he'd ever been in his life. All the way back to the picket line he was congratulated, thumped in the back and told he was going to be better than his Da. By the time they'd tied up the pony and returned to the trap he almost felt as if he'd actually won the race. There he was hugged by his granny, had his hand almost squashed by Martin, and was nodded at by a foolish, smiling, drunken Jobber. He ate voraciously, with an appetite he'd thought he'd completely lost. At about the same time Tom was half a mile from the crowd, looking back, admiring the colourful spectacle. He was warming up the brown in preparation for the race. He watched as a two-wheeled cart was drawn out from the gathering. This would be the half-way marker for the big race. It would be a mile, the cart being settled eight-hundred-and-fifty yards from the starting line. He cantered back towards the crowd.

Joe rode out to meet him on the piebald. Side by side, they approached the track. Joe was saying 'There's only two to watch. The big roan and the black with the Arab blood. Mostly the black. That's the one with the speed. The guy riding him is a complete dirty bastard. Watch him.'

'Okay' was Tom's terse reply.

The steward called for the line-up. Tom ended up on the right edge. With the whistle they all started in a line. For the length of the enclosed track they all kept apace. Hitting the open ground the roan moved into the lead and several followed. Tom speeded up a little but didn't attempt to catch up yet. The black moved forward. Tom was passing the rest of the field easily, and when he reached the turn he was fifth. The roan was still in the lead but the black was moving into second place. Time to move, Tom told himself, and gave the brown his heels. He bent low over the neck and spoke urgently into the ear of the brown. He spurted forward. Ahead, the black took the lead. Tom urged the brown past the remaining few between him and the black. Entering the enclosed track he passed the roan, gaining all the time on the black. He knew now he could take him, but so did the rider on the black. Tom was on the right side of the track. The black, nearer the middle, suddenly swerved to the right. He hoped to run the brown into the carts, but even as the black was changing direction so also was Tom. He turned the brown sharply to the left, passing the rump of the black by inches. As he made the pass he gripped the brown with his thighs and holding the mane with his left hand he grabbed the tail of the black and pulled sharply, letting the momentum of the black's sharp left turn, combined with the pull exerted on its tail, bring the animal completely around. It came around too fast to hold its footing and so collapsed onto its left side, throwing the rider clear between the back and front wheels of a four-wheeled cart.

Tom in the meantime had crossed the finish line, followed by the roan. He dismounted quickly, handed his reins to the nearest spectator and ran back along the side to the fallen animal. After a quick look he hauled it to its feet and led it along the side past the finishing line. These reins he handed to another spectator. Never once had he even glanced at the fallen rider.

He saw that Joe had the reins of the brown, so he approached the steward who pulled him up on the cart he was using as a platform. He handed Tom the prize money, and taking the hand clutching the money held it above Tom's head in the manner of a victorious boxer. The crowd roared their appreciation of a very exciting race. Tom's hand was nearly torn off him in congratulations on his way to the picket line.

He drank thirstily from a flagon of cider someone had handed him.

'That was some move, Tom,' Joe said. 'Where did you learn that one?'

'In Mountjoy,' Tom answered.

Before he could ask Tom to explain they were surrounded by people giving them money.

Between the prize money and the betting the brothers were considerably richer. Joe decided to go dicker for the palomino. Tom returned to the trap hungry now after the race. Martin and the Jobber were delightfully drunk. His mother fed him and they talked awhile.

'Your Da made a packet on the race,' his mother told him. 'In fact, I made a few pounds myself.'

'You enjoying the day, Ma?' he asked her.

'Oh, it was great Tom, especially watching young Tommy. He did well, didn't he?'

'Very well, Ma,' Tom assured her. 'He'll be winning from here on out.'

'Joe told me about the stallion, Tom,' she confessed. 'Will there be trouble?'

'I hope not, Ma,' he said. Sensing more, he asked, 'Why ask me that now?'

'Some travellers gave your father a message for you,' she told him. 'Walter wants to see you tomorrow. He expects to have the information for you then.'

'Good,' Tom said simply.

'Tom, there's something else.'

'What's that, Ma?'

'I saw you and Marie when Tommy was starting that race. You could do a lot worse.'

Tom said 'I'm going to find Joe. There's a mare we're interested in. See you in a while.'

'I'll probably be gone home, Tom. I'm getting tired and I don't fancy spending the evening with this pair of drunken old farts. One of our neighbours offered me a lift home in his car. Enjoy yourself son.'

'Okay. Ma, see you later.'

Joe was at the picket line, showing off their new mare.

'She's a beaut, Tom, is she not?' Joe was drunk.

Tom agreed. 'What did you give for her?' he asked.

'The piebald and a hundred and fifty,' he replied proudly.

'You did well, Joe,' Tom told him. He added, 'Walter wants to see me tomorrow.'

'Ah,' Joe said, 'we'd better get drunk tonight so.'

Three hours later Tommy proudly drove the trap in the fading evening. Behind him rode a cowboy and an Indian, arms around each others' shoulders, sharing a bottle of fire-water and engaged in incoherent conversation, content to let the ponies do the thinking.

Chapter 9

After breakfast the next morning, Martin, the Jobber and Joe took the trap and the animals back to Cold Cut. Tom had an appointment with Walter Small. Walking towards Labre Park he felt a great relief. Something at last was happening. Almost two weeks of suppressing his feelings had been as bad as being in prison again.

Walter's daughter let him in. She prepared tea as before, and left the two alone.

'Hello, Tom,' Walter began.

'Good to see you Walter,' Tom replied.

'I heard you had great success at the racing. There is much talk of your tailing the black. It's small wonder you have enemies.' Walter laughed.

'Yes, it was a great day. Profitable too. Joe acquired a fine palomino mare. With the stallion she should have some interesting foals.'

'Ah, the stallion.'

'You found him?' Tom enquired.

'Yes, we think so.'

'Where?'

'Foxrock.'

'Foxrock!' Tom said incredulously. 'What the fuck is he doing in Foxrock?'

'I will explain,' Walter said. 'Do you know of the Harcourt Line?'

'Disused railway line,' Tom replied. 'Went from Harcourt Street to Bray, I think.'

'That's right,' Walter told him. 'It passed through many of the suburbs on the way. Foxrock included.' He continued, 'The tracks were removed, even the bridges were pulled

37

down. What remains now is a strip of overgrown land. Our people, as you know well Tom, miss very little. This strip of land teems with much that is saleable. People use it as a dump. It passes by their back gardens. Where there's muck, there's money. Scrap metal, usable items that can be sold, we sift through it regularly.

Walter poured tea before continuing.

'Wild things are plentiful, rabbits and pheasant, our young boys enjoy to hunt and snare. Two such boys were hunting pheasant behind the big houses in Foxrock. These particular houses have very big gardens that back onto the line. Some of them have old buildings at the ends of the gardens that were used as stables in the old days. From one of these the lads heard the sounds of a horse. They were able to peep in. All they could tell was that it was a chestnut. A big chestnut. There were no windows or anything at the back. All were newly blocked up. That's all we knew then, the house and a horse. One of the women that begs from door to door in that area told us that the people who lived there were ordinary Dublin people, not gentry like the rest. There are other things. Four men and one woman live there. One of the cars there is a blue Mercedes. One of the men is called Dermot McMurragh.'

Tom exclaimed 'The Cur, the Cur McMurragh.'

'So,' Walter said, 'you know him.'

'Yes,' Tom replied. 'I went to school with him, but I haven't spoken to him for seven or eight years. I seem to remember him about two years ago in Ballyfermot.'

'He lives in Foxrock. What does he do?' Walter wanted to know.

'While I was in the Joy, I met a guy from Ballyer said he'd worked for the Cur. He said that he was one of the big heroin suppliers.'

'A rotten business,' Walter said sadly. 'Some of our young people have been affected. Has he some reason to do you harm?'

'None that I know of,' Tom said, remembering. 'I beat the shit out of him at school, as a matter of fact, a few times. Jesus, Walter, we were about ten at the time. Schoolyard gangs. I met him since and we had the crack about those times.'

'We still don't know if it's your stallion Tom,' Walter

pointed out.

'That's true, but it looks very much like it is. There are too many coincidences. I'll need some help to find out. I know nothing about that area at all. Can one of those boys show me the place. That's all I'll want. I'm not involving your people in whatever happens after that.'

'That is good, Tom,' Walter agreed. 'I will arrange this today. Word will be sent to your house later. I will try and have a car pick you up tomorrow morning with someone who will know that area. They will show you whatever you need to know.'

'I'm in your debt, Walter,' Tom told him.

'Think nothing of it, my son,' Walter said. 'Besides, we made a lot of money on you on Sunday.'

'Why?' Tom asked himself as he walked away from Labre Park. 'Why?'

He had no doubt that the chestnut horse was his stallion. He and the Cur had been rivals, but that was nearly twenty years ago. It was kids' stuff. They'd had rival gangs in the schoolyard. There must have been twenty such gangs. All these gangs had fought one another at some stage. Just like in the American pictures – the Blackboard Jungle. It was all the go. Stone wars. How many times had they been stitched. How many cuts had they not bothered getting stitched. He still met fellas from those wars and they, like him, had boys as old as they were when they were doing it. The Cur ran a gang then. He'd had about eight loyal followers. Tom tried to remember them. Come on, Tom told himself. This is stupid. Tomorrow you'll go suss it out and you'll do whatever you have to. Now you'll go for a pint.

That's what he did. He chose the County Bar. On his second pint a guy he'd gone to school with came in. They talked pleasantly about old times. Yeah, he remembered the Cur but hadn't seen him for years. He'd heard he was living in a big house in Foxrock.

Dermot McMurragh. He was known as 'The Cur' but very few people said it to his face. In looks he was the opposite of what you'd expect. He looked like a rugby player in the Tony O'Reilly mould, like a health-conscious barrister. Six three, blond, blue-eyed, sixteen stone, with no fat. And he dressed the part. Berber jacket and the cavalry twills. He was a successful criminal in that he'd never spent a day in prison.

After school, in fact while he was at school, he took to robbing gas meters. This was considered a pretty low crime, stealing from the people who could least afford it, who themselves had to replenish the money stolen. The little money he acquired this way was enough to be the Big Lad dispensing largesse among the loyal members of his little gang from school. He initiated them into the life. It didn't take long until he was fencing for them. In effect they were now working for him and grateful to do it. As his fencing operation became more efficient he could handle more and more stuff, so he began planning jobs for his gang and others to do. He was good at it.

Around that time he gained the attention of one Dumbo Deegan, a big-eared detective. Deegan recruited the Cur as his personal nark, immunity for information. This association proved advantageous for both parties. The future looked good for the Cur. He married a very pretty girl from Ballyfermot and bought a house there. He bullied her as he had his mother. His mother had retaliated by quietly robbing him blind, his wife by playing around. His vanity was such that when told of these things, to tell him proved so dangerous that very soon nobody did.

History took a hand in his career. Cannabis moved from the hippy pad to the house in the suburbs and what a lovely business. The Cur moved into the pharmaceutical line. He himself discovered this hash had a very pleasant effect. The Irish were developing a drug awareness. The Cur got into heroin almost by accident. For a period in 1979 no hash could be had for love nor money. At the same time heroin was available for little or nothing. He decided to try moving a little.

It was a dream. Customers literally screaming for it and junkies by the hundred dying to take all the risk of distribution. Within a year he'd a house in Foxrock, bought and paid for, money it was taking a lot of energy to bury. He was successful enough to be offered a seat on the Board of Directors, the Godfathers of importation and distribution of heroin in Ireland. He had it made. Smack was a loser's drug. He would not be foolish enough to try it, but he did develop a little predilection for cocaine.

He lived in luxury in his house in Foxrock with his wife and at least three of his most trusted men. In the renovated stables at the end of his garden was Tom Reid's stallion.

To pass the afternoon Tom volunteered to do a job Joe had intended to do. Driving one of the carts, he moved some furniture from Inchicore to Ballyfermot. On his return he was greeted with the message that a car would call for him at ten the following morning.

'Do you have any idea how you'll handle it?' Joe asked him later over a drink.

'Just that I take my stallion back,' Tom said. 'How I do it, I'll figure out after I've looked the place over.'

'I know it goes against the grain, but have you thought about going to the police?' Joe asked.

'Yeah, I thought about it,' Tom confessed, 'but if you look at it, no papers on the stallion and my word against a businessman in Foxrock. Me just out of the nick.'

'I wonder do the cops know what he does?' Joe wondered.

'I'm sure they do, but knowing it and proving it are two different things.'

'Do you want me to go along?'

'Thanks Joe,' Tom answered. 'Tomorrow I'll check it out, see how I can handle it, maybe I'll need you. I hope I don't. One of us in trouble is enough, okay.'

'It's as much my business as yours. That's what I'm saying.'

'Thing that bothers me most,' Tom said, 'is that I don't know why. When you know why a man does something, then you understand him a little. You can guess what he might do next. It's a slight edge.' He paused . . . 'Fuck him anyway!'

Chapter 10

A Hiace van picked Tom up next morning. He wore a woollen hat, his hair tucked under it.

'Billy Ward,' the driver introduced himself. 'It's a pleasure to help. You might not remember me, but we stopped together in Clonmel when you travelled with the Smalls.'

'Was it you had the Lurcher?' Tom asked.

'Yeah, I traded him for a transistor radio after. Damned thing never worked right.'

They drove for a while in silence.

Billy broke the silence. 'What do you want to do, Tom?'

'I have to see the horse first, make sure it's mine,' Tom told him.

'Right so' Billy said. 'We'd better approach from the back. I'll park in the car park of Leopardstown Racecourse. They won't notice the van there. We'll walk across the course to the old railway line. It's a common sight people walking that way. They can't see us from the house on account of the trees. I just don't want to arouse any suspicions. You probably won't want to be remembered by anybody afterwards.'

Billy parked the van behind the clubhouse. There were several other vans there, workmen and deliverymen. They aroused no interest. Walking across the course they were passed by several people. It was a popular short-cut. There was about four hundred yards of open level ground before they reached the site of the old railway line. The remains of the old railway station stood on the far side of the line. A few yards beyond the station was a shop. Billy pointed down the line to their right indicating where they had to go. He told Tom to sit on what was the old platform and wait. He went into the shop and returned with two choc ices. They sat eating in the warm sun. Picking a moment when nobody was nearby they strolled casually towards the back of the house. Within yards they were out of sight in the undergrowth. Relaxed now they walked the hundred yards to the old stables. Billy pointed to a narrow space between two blocks. Tom peered through for a while before he made the clicking noise with his tongue. The excited whinny from inside confirmed the presence of the stallion. Tom spoke softly through the gap and the stallion quietened.

'There's no way in from here,' Tom observed, 'short of knocking the wall.'

Billy pointed to the overgrown state of the garden to the left. 'You should be able to see the front of the stable from there without being seen yourself.'

Tom melted into the bushes. He was gone about five minutes. Billy was smoking a cigarette when he emerged. He offered Tom one and lit it for him.

'There's only a bolt on the door to the stable, no lock. I got close enough to see the same arrangement on the side gate. It would be simple to get in from this garden to the stable and out the side gate to the road, but then what?'

Billy said, 'This is not like Ballyer here, riding a horse bareback in the middle of the night would be a bit unusual. These people get a lot of looking after by the law as well. You wouldn't last a mile on the road.'

'This old line here,' Tom asked. 'How far is it passable?'

'I'm not sure, but it goes all the way to Ranelagh,' Billy told him.

'If I could get on to the canal from there I could make it. Can we take a look around the front of the house?' Tom asked.

'Sure.' Billy said. 'We'll go back and get the van and drive around.'

It was a good twenty minutes before they parked the van opposite the Cur's house. They sat there for fifteen minutes. Nobody came or went. Tom measured the distance from the house to the entrance to the old station. He guessed it was not much more than a hundred yards.

'Thanks for your help.' Tom and Billy shook hands. They were back at Tom's house.

'Good luck!' Billy told him. 'If you need me again, for

anything, just tell Walter.'

Tom thanked him again and Billy drove off.

Later, when Joe arrived home, Tom enquired 'Can you get your hands on a motor?'

'Sure,' his brother said. 'I borrow one now and then.'

'Can you get one for tomorrow night?' Tom asked.

'I'd say so,' Joe assured him.

Tom explained the situation to him and told him his plan.

'I'll only need you to drive me there. If for any reason I decide not to go ahead I'll need to be driven away. I don't fancy taking taxis out there to discover it can't be done that night, taking another home, and so on and so on. If I decide to do it then you just drive away, understood?'

Joe wondered if there wasn't anything else he could do.

'No!' Tom emphasised. 'You just have to get me there and away if necessary. The rest is a one-man job. There's nothing more you can do.'

Chapter 11

The next day began as a normal working day. Breakfast, a couple of hours chopping logs, scrap collection and lunch. In the afternoon Tom bought a good torch and visited Tommy at his mother's. They talked awhile but the boy left to play a match, leaving his parents alone. They sat in awkward silence for a while.

Marie spoke first. 'There's something going on Tom. What is it?'

'It doesn't concern you Marie,' Tom insisted.

Marie began angrily, 'I smell trouble Tom and trouble for you affects Tommy. That makes it my business. He worships you and he just spent a year of his life without you. These are very important years.'

She softened. 'In the name of God, Tom, please tell me what's going on.'

Tom thought for a moment, then slowly began to speak. He told Marie everything. He was surprised how much better he felt after putting it into words, all of it, not just what was happening, but his feelings about what was happening. With Joe, his earnest friend, his brother, from whom he withheld nothing, it was not the same. Man to man it was the resolving of a problem, rationally. Essential, certainly, but with Marie . . . .

'Jesus Christ,' he thought, 'I'm twenty-six years old. Is this the first time I've ever spoken to a woman?'

Marie watched him closely, seeing him as never before. Exposed. This quiet, tough man, showing confusion and apprehension, even fear. Normal fear. Something gave inside of her. She began to cry softly, sadness for all those years not knowing him, happiness that she finally should.

He moved so quietly she didn't realise he had, until her face was in his hands as he kissed away her tears. Infinitely slowly, as if an awkward movement might shatter the spell, she took his hand and led him up the stairs. In the bedroom he stood shyly as she undressed him, shedding her own clothes as she drew him into her bed. Making love, his unexpected patience and gentleness drew from her a passion that surprised and excited him. They lay side by side for a long time in contented silence.

Marie said suddenly, 'Tom, we'd better get up, Tommy will be home any minute.'

'No,' Tom told her, 'let him find us as we are.'

Some minutes later Tommy burst into the bedroom shouting 'Ma'. Seeing Tom he said, 'Howya Da. Ma, I'm not having tea. I'm going over to Ted's house to watch a video. See yis.' He was gone. They both laughed, Tom almost to the point of hysterics. He tried to remember when was the last time he had laughed like that.

In the kitchen, Marie asked, referring to the stallion, 'Is there any chance you could just forget this?'

Tom didn't answer. Looking at him she conceded, 'No, how could you.'

She paused and spoke again. 'There's something I think you need to know. It might be part of the "Why" that bothers you.'

She continued, 'When Tommy was three, I went out for about six weeks with Dermot McMurragh. I was lonely. He was good-looking and attentive and it was good for me for a while. For all that, I realized quickly that I didn't like him. When I told him I wasn't going out with him anymore, he asked me to marry him. I said no. As I said, it only lasted six weeks, seven years ago, but it's something else that connects him with you.'

'Yeah,' Tom said distractedly. 'Thanks for telling me.'

Marie busied herself around the house. Tom sat considering the web that threaded through his life and the Cur's, but like a web, it lacked tangibility, the gut. He shrugged off the useless conjecture. 'Marie,' he called, 'I gotta go.' When she came he explained, 'Joe'll be waiting.'

She kissed him. 'Be careful.'

When he arrived home, outside the house was an old Escort

van. Inside Joe was eating. Tom joined him.

'See the motor?' Joe asked.

Tom, eating, nodded.

'What time do you want to leave?' enquired Joe.

'No hurry,' Tom told him, 'I won't be doing anything till they're settled down in the house. We'll have a few pints somewhere like Rathmines, have a hamburger or something after closing time, then head for Foxrock.'

'Will we need anything?' Joe wanted to know. He was nervous.

'I got a good torch today. We'll take a bridle,' Tom told him, 'and for God's sake relax.'

They left the house at nine thirty and drove to Rathmines. After closing time they crossed the road and passed an hour and a half in one of the many cafés. It was nearing two a.m. when they reached Foxrock. Tom directed Joe so that they could pass the house going in the direction of the old station. Passing the house they slowed down. Tom scrutinised the front of the darkened house. There were four cars in the driveway.

'Pull in here,' Tom directed Joe into the short cul-de-sac of the old station. 'Turn the van and park.'

Tom lit a cigarette, giving Joe his final instructions.

'I'm going in the back way. If all goes well I go out the front and come back this way. As soon as I leave you now, you pull out and park on the street. Watch the road both ways. Round here people don't walk around at night, so it'll be cars you're watching. Don't do anything for ten minutes. Time it. After that, anything comes, beep once, second beep means they're gone. Okay?'

'Right,' Joe said.

'When I go by you, then you take off,' Tom finished.

They shook hands and Tom disappeared into the darkness.

Chapter 12

In among the bushes Tom used the torch till he reached the rear of the house next door, then doused it. For about two minutes he stood still allowing himself to become accustomed to the dark. He picked his way gingerly through the bushes until he was level with the front of the stable. Stock still, he examined the back of the Cur's house. All was dark and quiet. As he climbed into the Cur's garden, he made soft quietening sounds for the stallion. He eased the bolt back slowly on the stable door. The almost inaudible noise it made sounded tremendous to Tom's alert hearing. He slipped into the stable, pulling the door after himself. In the darkness he spoke softly to the stallion. Its huge head found Tom's hand. He lovingly stroked it until he was sure of the animal's confidence. He slipped the bridle over the animal's head.

Opening the door slightly, he again perused the house and garden. All was as before. He emerged with the stallion and led him slowly towards the gate at the side of the house. Again, the sliding bolt sounded deafening. It wasn't. He walked the stallion to the street entrance. Here he was clothed in shadow. He peered around the gate-post in the direction where Joe was parked. All was clear. He walked from the garden towards the cul-de-sac. No traffic. Joe watched him through the rear window of the van. Once in the cul-de-sac he mounted the stallion. They turned onto the old railway line and melted into the darkness. Tom flicked on the torch and a trail opened up dimly ahead. Though he was passing through the heart of the suburbs he might have been in a narrow valley in the wildest part of the country. The sides rose steeply on either side. The young trees and bushes opened before him and closed behind him. No sound, no light reached him from the houses a stone's throw to the left and the right of him. Startled birds took flight, disturbed animals fled, rustling through the brush. Dogs barked, cats screamed, once he heard the question Whoo? Whoo? asked by an inquisitive owl.

The stallion was restive. Tom presumed he'd had no exercise during his captivity. Several times he had to dismount when the trail disappeared. On these occasions he found he could pass by moving up the slope on one side or the other. Danger was present in the shape of old rusted bicycle frames, bed springs, pram frames. These he had to clear from the trail to protect the stallion's legs. Time lost all meaning. Distance covered was impossible to compute. Twice Tom found he had to leave the stallion and climb up from the line where it had been filled in to provide access across it. The first time he simply found a way over the infilling and back down on the other side. The second time he had to break through fencing on either side of the access and lead the stallion through the gaps.

It was coming first light when he reached the third obstacle. He climbed the slope to find he had come to a point where the old line had been built on. He could follow it no further. He was not sure where he was. He guessed it was the back of Ranelagh. When he returned to the horse it was munching away contentedly, so Tom took the opportunity to have a smoke. The day lightened as he sat. The wild creatures grew accustomed to the two intruders. Birdsong filled the air and the undergrowth rustled as the small four-leggeds hustled in the new day. The ants finally tickled Tom from his reverie. He took the stallion's reins and led him up to the street. On the bare back of the chestnut, Tom nudged him forward. Turning the first corner the stallion almost stood on the shiny black shoes of a uniformed guard. Tom controlled the startled stallion.

The young guard stood, hands on hips, considering the spectacle before him. He eventually spoke. 'Geronimo,' he said, smiling at his own wit, then added, 'Sir, would you be so kind as to dismount.'

Tom slid down. 'Where might you be going?' the guard initiated enquiries.

'Home' Tom told him.

'Where might that be?'

'Ballyfermot' was Tom's reply.

'I had a feeling that you were not from around here,' the Guard observed. 'Your horse?'

The guard bent and looked under the horse. 'Stallion!' he corrected himself. The guard was having a ball.

'Is it, Guard?' Tom asked.

'Funny,' said the officer, 'it fits the description of a stallion reported missing from Foxrock in the early hours of this morning.'

At that Tom realised there was no point in feeding lines to an aspiring comedian, so he remained silent.

The guard was in no way put off. 'Do you realize that you're my first rustler. Luckily for you it's not a hanging offence in the Ranelagh-Rathmines area. Do you want to tell me your name.'

'Tom Reid.'

The guard regarded him awhile. 'You were nicked last year over another horse. There were a lot of us didn't think you should have gone down.' He paused before continuing. 'I can get the squad car, or you can walk with me to the station. We can't put the horse in the squad car.'

'Let's walk,' Tom replied.

As they walked the guard was thinking. 'You're saying that somebody in Foxrock stole the stallion from you?'

'Yeah.'

'You can see how that would be hard to believe,' the guard told him.

'That's why I just took it back. I couldn't go to the police, could I?' Tom said.

'Let's see what happens when we get to the station,' the guard finished.

They walked in silence to the police station at Rathmines. At the back of the station a place was found to tether the stallion. Tom was then led inside. The desk sergeant questioned the arresting guard.

'What have we here?'

'A joy rider,' the guard told him.

Tom provided them with his name and address, and was then led to a small room in the back. He was left alone. Tea was provided for him almost immediately. He sat for several hours, interrupted at regular intervals by some guard or detective curious to see the first horse thief in the history of the Rathmines manor.

Later the door opened and the guard who'd arrested him entered, accompanied by a man in civilian clothes. Tom recognised him.

'Hello Dumbo,' Tom addressed him, much to the amusement of the guard.

'Detective Deegan to you, laddie,' was the unhappy reply.

'He claims the stallion is his,' the guard informed the detective.

The detective laughed derisively and said, 'This here is a known convicted criminal from Ballyfermot.' He laughed mockingly, 'Tonto Reid. That horse belongs to Mr. Dermot McMurragh, a business man, a resident of Foxrock. It was reported missing at three o'clock this morning. At seven it was discovered in the possession of this man here. An open and shut case as far as I'm concerned.'

The uniformed guard interjected, 'Isn't McMurragh also from Ballyfermot?' implying a possible connection between the two men. If Deegan was aware of the inference he chose to ignore it.

'Indeed he was,' the detective agreed, 'but unlike this person, he improved his station through his diligence and his business expertise, and now holds a highly responsible position in this city. Enough of this, I've wasted more time on this miserable case than it's worth.' He left the room.

The guard produced cigarettes and lit one each for himself and Tom.

'Despite what Deegan says,' the guard began, 'we're all aware of McMurragh's business. Unfortunately we've never been able to build a case against him. He manages to keep himself about three steps removed from the actual handling of drugs. Incidentally, what does he want with your horse? He could afford to buy a racehorse.'

Tom replied, 'He's trying to get on my wick for some reason. I've known him since National School, and that's the last time I had any dealings with him.'

'He's a strange man, Tom,' the guard said, 'I know some of the guys who keep surveillance on him. He rarely leaves the house. Goes out to eat now and then or for a business meeting with the other big suppliers. That's about it. Keeps at least three of his lads in the house with him all the time. There's a dozen that do it in shifts, just like a factory. His missus goes out all the time. He doesn't seem to have much fun with all the money he's making.'

'Why are you telling me all this?' Tom wanted to know.

'Firstly, I checked to see if you had a record. Besides the usual kids' stuff there's nothing against you except that assault against those punks that tortured the pony. And I already said most of the cops I know felt you should have got a medal for that. Secondly, I'm a guard and I passionately hate smack. It not only destroys people, it creates criminals. Dangerous criminals, with no sense of proportion. People who will kill or maim for a tenner. Psychopaths.' He lit two more cigarettes before continuing. 'Now the Cur, one of the biggest suppliers in Dublin, steals your stallion, a beautiful animal, but no thoroughbred. What I'm saying is that it wasn't for gain. It seems like an act of petty spite. It's stupid. I think like a cop. Is he slipping, is this a way to get at him?' he paused. 'Can you prove you own the stallion?'

'I've nothing on paper, if that's what you mean,' Tom told him.

'Well, can you produce people in court who can tesitfy for you. Whoever you bought it from, for instance?' the guard suggested.

'I traded for his mother when I was a kid and had her covered. I could bring fifty people who would swear that I've had that stallion for nearly ten years. People who have known me all that time, would that do?' Tom asked.

'It might,' the guard said. 'Now we'll see if he is going to charge you.' The guard left.

Tom sat alone for another hour, before the guard returned.

'McMurragh is not charging. You're free,' Tom was told. 'But the stallion goes back to Foxrock.'

'I see,' Tom said.

'What will you do now?' the guard asked him.

'I don't know . . .' Tom confessed, 'I don't know.'

'Whatever you decide Tom, look me up if you need any help,' the guard told him. 'Ask for Vinny O'Dowd.'

The men shook hands and Tom left the station.

Chapter 13

At the house Joe waited anxiously for his brother's return.

'What the hell happened?, Joe asked, seeing Tom without the stallion. Tom filled him in.

'Jesus!' Joe exclaimed, 'Is Deegan just stupid or is he playing the old soldier?'

'He's the Cur's man,' Tom told him, 'and I think the other guards have that much sussed.'

'We're really up against it.' Joe sighed. 'What the hell can we do?'

'Do about what?' It was the voice of Martin. 'What could it be that has the pair of ye so goddamned miserable?' he demanded to know.

Tom started to explain. After a bit Martin interrupted.

'This conversation is not one I'd want your mother interrupting, so let's adjourn to the office.'

He led them to the shed, and closing the door he produced a bottle from one of his many hiding places. He took a healthy slug and said 'Sobriety has a terrible way of stifling the imagination and by the sounds of this problem we need all the brain-power we can muster.'

Passing the bottle to Tom he said 'Talk away son. Tell me all about it.' Tom drank and then spoke. By the time he finished they were near the end of the bottle. The father considered for quite a while before speaking.

'Knowing you, Tom, I can safely say that you're not about to drop the matter.'

Tom nodded his head in reply.

'Well now,' the Da began, 'we have here a very powerful man with powerful friends, a mighty adversary. But as the old cliché goes, the bigger they come, etcetera. For every man has

53

a weak spot boys. This is what ye must do. Get inside the whore's head and think like a whore. Then slowly, deliberately and with sweet pleasure break his fucking black heart!'

'God,' Joe said, feigning surprise, 'you are an evil old man.'

Martin spoke proudly, 'My ancestors, and yours, many years ago, came up against a fella by the name of Cromwell. This particular bastard took their good land and banished them "To hell or to Connaught". To the most godforsaken, begrudging, barren, heart-breaking place on this island. To hell, boys. One of the few advantages of surviving in Hell is that you get to know the divil. Divilment is part of life. A decent enemy deserves every bit of evil you can think up.'

The brothers were stunned to silence. The Da rooted out another bottle. The shock of another mouthful of his father's moonshine brought Tom back to life.

'Da,' he said, 'getting into the bastard's head is the hard part. Sure we still haven't figured what the hell he is doing this for in the first place.'

'Ah,' replied Martin, 'in a case like this, you need the services of a reputable informer, and' said he, 'before ye ask me who, I'll tell ye. There is a lad who used to live just down the street, whom you lads went to school with, who is the driver for the Cur McMurragh, and from what I hear, is the confidant of the same Cur. In case you don't understand French, your man tells him everything.'

'Why would *he* tell *us* anything?' Joe asked.

'Because,' said Martin, 'his mother is very fond of and beholden to your mother. Tonight I will tell your mother to have a little word with her. Now boys, if you have no further need of my wisdom I will grab a biteen of dinner before joining my friends at the pub.'

Both of them more than a little drunk, Tom asked Joe 'Did he walk out that door without a wobble?'

'He did,' Joe admitted.

'Did you hear that son of a bitch?' Tom asked.

'I did.'

'It's that easy?'

'So it seems.'

'Fuck me!'

Joe staggered into the house, waving vaguely. Tom

wandered into the yard. He walked in by the mare in the shed. She stood chewing. Solid, placid. She had water, enough grain, herself. Tom sat back against the wall, against a smooth piece of concrete, counting the few stars.

A cup of tea was in his hand. Tasting it, he became aware of it. His mother stood before him.

'Away with the fairies son?' she whispered.

The boy nodded.

'Da says you need to talk to Benny.'

Tom swallowed another mouthful of tea. 'Yes, Ma.' He controlled his speech. 'It could be a big help.'

'I'll see to that,' she told him. 'You better come in and eat before the other two finish it all, 'cos I'm going out soon.'

Tom accepted her hand. She braced him as he pushed himself up. They walked side by side into the house. Tom's hunger surprised him, or maybe the ribs boiled with cabbage and the potatoes with the butter were just so good. After the food he drank cup after cup of hot strong tea, until his imagination came to earth. His mother and father left and Joe snored on the couch. Eventually Tom felt steady enough to venture out. He walked as far as Marie's, taking the longest route. Tommy met him at the door and ushered him in.

'How did you get on?' Marie enquired.

Tom detailed the events of the previous twenty hours. It occurred to him that it seemed a lot longer than a mere day. He finished by saying: 'Now I do as my father says, scheme and plan until I can find some way to get at him. Talk to as many people as I can that know him. It looks like I'm going to have to be patient again for a while.'

Tom stayed the night, the first of many he would spend with the mother of his son.

Chapter 14

After his thwarted attempt to retrieve his stallion, Tom's life resumed its normal pattern. But he was now willing to interrupt any task to converse with anyone who could tell him anything relating to the Cur or his activities. Tom's previous trouble with the authorities had attracted a lot of media coverage. He was a man who had spent a year in prison for doing something that most people hoped they would be capable of doing in similar circumstances. His neighbourhood was in a sense a large village, word of mouth still the most important medium of broadcasting local news. An already wronged man whose most prized and valuable possession is taken from him by a powerful and greedy gangster, a drug baron, Tom had a lot of sympathetic supporters. Actually it was getting embarrassing. In the local pubs it became impossible for him to pay for a drink.

Information, real or fancied, was offered at such a rate that he could have used a secretary to file it. More and more he became aware of an aspect of the neighbourhood he had known existed but had never really looked at before — drugs. Hash he was familiar with. Most of his friends used it. He'd used it himself many times. Glue-sniffing was popular among the younger crowds as indeed were cider, wine, hash and some pills. Heroin, however, he had seen little of. An old school friend approached him one afternoon as he was driving one of the carts.

'Remember me, Tom?' he asked.

'Billy Ryan,' Tom remembered. 'How are you doing?'

'Grand' he told Tom.

They reminisced awhile, but Billy soon turned to the subject of drugs. Of the fifty or so lads in their class at school, Billy named four who'd died of heroin-related causes. Two overdoses, one poisoned, the fourth killed in a robbery he'd been part of to pay for his habit. Billy named three more who were strung out, one of them lucky enough to be undergoing a cure.

'The other two are dealing,' Billy said. 'Smack that's coming from the Cur. They are dealing it here in Ballyfermot.'

'You seem to be well informed?' Tom asked.

'I have to be, Tom,' he explained. 'My eldest boy, same age as your own, came home one night out of his box. I shook it out of him. He'd snorted some smack he was given free by a guy up the street, one of my neighbours. I went straight up to his house, dragged him out and beat the bejasus out of him. I told him if one more kid in the street got anything from him again I'd swing for him. That same night six guys came to the door. I thought it was some heavies coming to sort me out for doing your man. I answered the door with the axe I use for chopping sticks. As it turned out it was six neighbours, whose kids had been offered stuff. That was the start of our committee. Pretty soon most of the parents on the road were involved. After that anyone dealing smack was told to stop it or move. Most moved. Some had to be convinced. They're all gone now, but they left a lot of junkies behind. We try to help them, figuring they could be any of us, but they still need to buy gear.'

'The dealers don't live around here now. They come in and out. As we were cleaning up our street, other streets were being sorted out the same way. Eventually all the street committees got together. Now we watch the whole scheme. There are groups like that all over the city now. We keep in touch and support each other if it's needed. The Cur is still the biggest supplier here, not that he goes door-to-door himself.'

Billy accepted Tom's tobacco and rolled himself a cigarette before he spoke again.

'I heard about you asking around about the Cur. I live on the same street as Marie. She knows where I am if you want me. I'm always there.'

'Thanks Billy,' Tom said, shaking his hand. Billy walked away. He had left Tom a lot to think about. How did the theft of a single horse compare to the deliberate destruction of young human life? The cold-blooded seduction of children, maybe even his own son, turned Tom's initial resentment to fear, and the determination to resolve. While he was helpless in prison his fatherly responsibilities were being assumed by people he hardly knew. With his gratitude came the realisation of his indebtedness. 'I didn't realise how serious it was,' he admitted to Marie later. 'If I'd known while I was locked up what was going on here on this street I'd have cracked up.'

'That was a bad time here,' Marie explained. 'We were all scared and unsure. It took a lot of time to believe it was really happening. All the talk and the guessing. The people who were supposed to be into it were people you knew, people you thought had some sense. There were so many on pills from the doctors that when they were stoned you figured it was the tranquillizers. Then suddenly one night there's Billy Ryan, one of the quietest fellas on the street, dragging this other man out of his house, shouting about smack and the kids. The other men had to stop him from doing murder. But after that it was all out in the open. We all knew. Then the job of getting rid of the pushers began. It was pretty rough for a month or two, but the people were together. It made this street, it made people aware. Now there are clubs and things organised for the kids. There are still a lot of people addicted, but they're to be pitied more than anything else.'

'Where are they getting their stuff now?' Tom asked.

'People come around.' Marie said. 'The Committee keep an eye on them, making sure they get no new customers, especially the kids. With all the lads on the dole here there's no shortage of people to watch them. They know all the junkies. If too many people start calling to their houses then they are visited by the Committee. If the Committee think they're dealing they call a meeting and it's discussed. Those suspected are entitled to defend themselves at the meeting. If the worst comes to the worst they are forced to move. Trouble is, some other area just ends up with the problem. All we can do is clean up our own streets and hope everybody does the same.'

Chapter 15

Benny the Wren Finnegan, the Cur's driver, turned up on Tom's doorstep, driving the Cur's blue Mercedes. The wren was tiny, five-two, a shaper. In a bigger man, this throwing of the shoulders from side to side was meant to project a jaunty, fearless image. With Benny people were reminded of the jerky nervous movements of a wren. 'This is the motor they used to lift your stallion,' he informed Tom, 'Exhibit A.' He laughed so infectiously at his own joke that Tom found himself laughing in spite of himself.

'Let's go for a spin,' he suggested. 'We'll burn some of the Cur's petrol.'

In the car, he drove sitting on a large cushion. 'Me Ma told me to come and see you,' he said, 'and I always do what me Ma tells me.'

Looking at him, and remembering the size of his mother, Tom wondered if he was really joking.

'When was the last time we seen each other?' Tom asked him.

'At least four years ago,' Benny guessed. 'That's it. When I brought my third young one to your house on her Communion day.'

Benny drove as far as the Strawberry Beds and stopped at the Strawberry Hall. 'We might as well have a pint while we talk.'

In the bar they took their pints to a seat by the wall. 'Well, Tom, me auld flower, what can I do for you?' he asked.

'I need to know what the fuck I did that the Cur has it in for me,' Tom told him.

'You got on television,' Benny answered. Benny purposely took a slow draught from his pint, enjoying Tom's confusion.

'I didn't know I was on television,' Tom admitted puzzled.

'You were,' the Wren assured him.

'Alright, so I was. I'll take your word for it. So what?' Tom asked.

'What everything!' Benny emphasized. 'Your being on television was the start of it.' Benny caught the barman's eye and signalled for two more pints. 'I'll explain.' Benny said. 'After you were sentenced, but before you started your term, Today Tonight did a programme about cruelty to animals. It was very good. Anyway, your case was highlighted. They explained the ins and outs of the case. While the talking was going on in the background the picture was you driving a cart around Ballyer.'

Tom interrupted, 'I remember now. They wanted to interview me and I said no. I couldn't stop them filming though. I completely forgot that.'

'Pity the Cur isn't as modest as you,' Benny commented. 'This shit would never have happened. There were five of us in the house in Foxrock that night. The Cur and his mot, me and two of his bodyguards. We were watching the programme.'

The barman brought the pints and the Wren paid for them before continuing. 'When they started to talk about you the rest of us got great crack outa somebody we knew being on the box. But when you came up on the screen, on the cart, the Cur really gets pissed off. He starts shouting "Look at that! Look at that! A fucking knacker and he gets a whole programme about himself on the television". He switches off the box and starts raving. "Look at me," he's shouting, "a successful businessman. Got myself out of Ballyfermot into a house in fucking Foxrock. I'm not on television." I says to him, look at the last lot in your business that got themselves on Today Tonight. They're either locked up or on the run. There's no talking to him. He's remembering what a bollocks you were in school and wouldn't marry that lovely girl you got in trouble. "I'll fix his wagon," he says and off he goes into his office. Soon as he was gone we stick the telly back on, but there's no more about you. They're on about greyhounds chasing hares. Anyway I figured that was the end of it, but a couple of months later he tells me to get somebody to fix up the sheds at the back. He's getting a horse, he says. It turns out he had some guy from Ballyer check you out and discovers you have a prize stallion that's your pride and joy, so he is going to rip it off just before you get out and really piss you off.'

Benny went to the gents and left Tom to absorb the story so far. He continued. 'That was his favourite part, you getting out of the nick to discover your most valuable asset just gone. Make your day. He must have spent weeks planning that, just so. Planning. Now he's excellent at that, always was. But he used to do his planning for break-ins, banks, security vans, constructive stuff. Now he puts the same precision into stealing a work horse, pardon the description, of some guy who outsmarted him in a game of cops and robbers when he was eight years old.'

'Are you telling me he's off his nut?' Tom asked.

'In one word,' the Wren said, 'Yes.'

'This is why he stays in the house all the time?' Tom suggested.

'More or less,' Benny replied. 'Getting into the drug business, moneywise, was a great move. After six months his organisation, with his usual brilliant planning, was running itself. All he had to do was count the money. This gets him a seat on the Board. He's accepted as an equal, with the biggest names in Irish crime. Two things happen here that fuck him up. One is that the rule of membership is no sidelines, nothing that might attract the attention of the law. No more setting up bank jobs, tasty little hijacks, worrying about the millions of little details of getting rid of two thousand videos, the things that keep him busy. Secondly, the favourite tipple of the board is champagne and coke, and I don't mean Coca Cola. This he takes to like a duck to water. I never tried the stuff meself, but it seems to change the way you look at things. Like a guy with twelve pints you meet when you're sober. The bould Cur is hitting this stuff morning, noon and night. He won't go to bed without a couple of grams on the bedside table – the way you or me need the bottle of lemonade after a night's drinking.'

Tom asked 'How come you're still with him?'

'I get four ton a week for being a driver,' the Wren explained. 'A chauffeur, that and listening to his bullshit. Work is hard to come by, Tom. I have a fair bit put by and I can't see the Cur lasting much longer. The way his head is he'll fuck up sooner or later. I'll see it out to the end. I'll tell you something else you may not believe. I like him. Behind all his big front, I still see the hungry kid we went to school with. If he had been born in the area he now lives in, he'd be successfully running an organisation as big as the one he's running now, but the end product would be legit. I think in his twisted way he sees you as successful in a way he isn't. You make a living and you have the one thing he hasn't, the respect of your neighbours. The only reason he gets respect is fear or some greedy swine trying to get something off him. Tom, as I said, I like him, but before you start to feel sorry for him, poor little rich boy, he hates your guts and the only reason he hasn't killed your horse is that he knows it annoys you more him just having it.'

Tom digested this.

'You reckon he's going to take a fall?' Tom asked.

'Stands to reason,' the Wren replied. 'If he doesn't give up the coke his loopiness must be copped by other heads on the board. Shit, they probably know already. The money involved is so fantastic they're not going to let him fuck it up. If they are wide to him already, the first time he puts a foot wrong, bang – they mightn't even wait.'

'In that light, taking my stallion could be a mistake for him?' Tom suggested.

'Definitely,' the Wren agreed. 'When they had you in Rathmines he wanted you charged. He figured you'd go down again. That's how much he likes you. That tells you he's not as bright as he was. One, you wouldn't have gone back in the nick, you've no form other than the assault. Second, a court case could've raised a lot of embarrassing questions. Dumbo Deegan talked him out of that. Now there's a gas situation, the cop keeping the Cur out of trouble. The lads think Deegan is in the Cur's pocket. He's not. He doesn't take a penny. The Cur is his nark. He's keeping the Cur in power thinking he'll save his shitty career with a big dramatic case against the Board. Never happen. Everyone of them is ten times removed from the smack.'

'What's my best move?' Tom asked him.

'Sit back the Wren told him. 'I already take care of the stallion. I'll see no harm comes to him. The Cur will fall, take my word for it.'

'He will indeed,' Tom agreed, without saying it.

The two men remained in the bar. The Wren dropped Tom back to his house. Sitting in the Merc, outside the house, he remarked: 'Remember what I told you. Just take it easy and let history take its course.'

'Sure,' Tom said, 'sure.'

Joe was chopping logs in the garden as Tom got out of the car. Tom joined him, filling him in as they worked.

'It's what I always said, Tom, when you appear on television, you become public property. Every punter thinks he owns a piece of you. The Cur chose your stallion.'

Chapter 16

Tom spent the next few days working and thinking. The information he had absorbed in the previous week tumbled about in his head, a stray idea spinning out here and there. Thinking was not Tom's favourite hobby, but his father's words egged him on, 'Scheme, plot, break his black fucking heart.' Eventually he ran his best ideas through the wringer and squeezed out the agonised few drops of a plan. He offered it up to Joe. 'This is what I figured so far,' he began. 'The old man said everyone has a weak spot. According to the Wren, the Cur's on is the Board. If they think he'll fuck them up, they'll sort him out and I'll get my stallion.'

Joe interrupted. 'How do you get the Board worried about him?'

'The Wren reckons they might be already,' Tom told him. 'I have to make them a little more worried.'

'You think you know how?' Joe enquired.

Tom nodded, saying, 'So far the Cur hasn't made any mistakes in his business dealings. It's his behaviour that niggles them. They may or may not know about the stallion. It's important how he reacted when I was held in Rathmines. He let his hatred for me overrule his usual better judgement. The real clincher is that this "hatred" is as a result of me being on the telly. That he risked a case which, with my previous telly exposure, isn't that what they call it, would have got me back on the telly. All because of a coke fantasy. The Board would freak out. A Today Tonight special.'

'You can't exactly apply for an interview with the Board,' Joe pointed out, 'and they don't hold shareholders meetings either. How do you inform the Board?'

'The way that would impress them the most,' Tom told him,

'I have to get back on the telly.'

'Tom,' Joe said, 'everybody wants to get on the telly. It's not that easy.'

'I'm going into showbusiness,' Tom proclaimed. 'I'm going to stage a "Horse Opera".'

'I think you've been on the coke,' Joe laughed. 'Give us an ould snort so I can get on the bandwagon.'

'It's the showbusiness drug,' Tom quipped.

'Okay, Tom, okay,' Joe said. 'Let's hear about the Horse Opera.'

'Horses are the thing that seem to be the cause of all this hassle. The poor old mare I got in trouble for in the first place, that got me on television. The stallion. I've been thinking, maybe a horse could be the answer. From what I've found out, the Cur's business is centred in Ballyer. His dealers come in and out all the time. I'm going to become the Lone Ranger.'

'Tonto, you mean, don't you?' Joe interjected.

Tom continued. 'I can start taking out the dealers on horse-back. One telephone call and surely the papers will pick that up. It makes a fine picture. They couldn't pass that up. If I can get in front of the cameras, he'll be out in no time. One interview and I broadcast direct to the Board. Everything I say can be verified. I'm in the book at Rathmines station for being caught with the stallion, yet no charges were made. I claim the stallion is mine and challenge him to prove otherwise in court. Getting to court doesn't really matter. Putting the spotlight on the Cur is the thing.'

'You have been on the coke,' Joe suggested. 'That's so fucking crazy it might even work.'

'To take out the dealers, now that's the problem. I need an organisation for that. I have to get on to them as soon as they hit the area,' Tom admitted. 'Such an organisation is already there. People who watch their every move. If they are willing to help me it can work, Joe, I know it can.'

'What about the law?' Joe asked. 'They mightn't like you doing their job.'

'I won't have to worry about them for a while,' Tom explained. 'It'll be a hit and run operation. If it comes together I won't even know till the last minute exactly where I'll be. Though I might have a few words with Vinny O'Dowd beforehand. The thing there is that no matter what, he is a cop and I don't know how far I can trust him.'

'What exactly will you do to the dealers?' Joe asked.

'Take their dope and money,' Tom answered. 'If I can get away with doing that for a week, there should be enough fuss to get the reaction I want, what do you think?'

'Sounds good, Tom,' Joe agreed, but at some stage the heavies will get involved, no?'

'I'm gambling on it taking a week before that happens,' Tom said. 'I mean, I just want to embarrass the Cur. I want to bring it home to the Board that the Cur is in danger of attracting the media.'

'What's the first move?' Joe enquired.

'Talk to Billy Ryan. See what he thinks. See will their organisation co-operate,' Tom explained. 'If it's on, you're going to have to take care of business on your own. I'll be otherwise engaged.'

'That's no problem,' Joe assured him. 'I handled that all last year.'

'Think like the bastard,' his father had said, and he was thinking like the Cur. Could anyone think like the Cur? Coked out.

Chapter 17

Marie was sceptical. 'Are you sure about this, Tom?' she asked.

'I gave it a lot of thought, Marie. I think it will work,' he told her.

'It's going to be dangerous. Most of the guys who deal for the Cur are junkies themselves. They can be pretty desperate, take chances that somebody else mightn't,' she warned.

'Marie,' he insisted, 'there's one thing I know for sure, I'm well able to handle myself. I'd love it if I could just call the Cur out and have a go, best man wins. Foxrock is a little different than Ballyer. I can't stand outside his house roaring "Come out, ye bollocks, and face me like a man." I'd be nicked in ten seconds flat. Marie, I wish it were that simple.'

'Tom, I know there's no way I can talk you out of this, but I'll be worried till it's over and done with.'

'Yeah,' Tom accepted, 'just remember that most city people are afraid of horses, especially if that horse is coming at twenty miles an hour. Ever see the mounted police in England the way they can handle a riot. It gives me a pretty good edge. With a bit of luck I'll only have to do it for a couple of days until the Board hears about it and wonders why. Once they figure out the Cur's side of it I reckon they are going to slap his hand. All I want is the stallion back. The Cur will fuck himself up sooner or later.'

'Suppose he freaks out and harms the stallion?' Marie asked nervously.

'I'm gambling on a couple of things there.' Tom explained. 'One, on the Wren cooling him just long enough for the Board to get the read. Two, the guys who run the rackets in the Joy. Those guys worked or work for people on that Board, judging by the amount of smack that was available in there. They know me as a dangerous amateur. They might figure it'd be easier to give me the goddamned horse and be rid of a nuisance.'

'They might not want to lose that much face,' Marie pointed out. 'Tom, I don't think you realise what you're up against. You're talking about millions of pounds. You can get killed in this town for fifty quid.'

'I thought about that Marie,' Tom admitted, 'but I'm tired of doing nothing. One of the most important things in my life was taken from me just because some twisted bastard thought it was funny. I can't do nothing, and still hold me head up. If he does harm that stallion then I'll get to him somehow and I'll tear his fucking head off.'

The lack of anger in Tom's voice, the naked violence of that matter-of-fact promise completely unnerved her. She put that beside the loving, tender man she was growing to love, and hoped to God she could learn to separate the two thereafter.

'Go now,' she said, 'please.'

Chapter 18

Billy Ryan laughed when Tom laid out his intentions. Tom couldn't tell if it was derision or glee.

'Why the hell not?' Billy laughed.

'You'll help?' Tom asked.

'Why the hell not!' Billy repeated. 'You'll be the one taking all the chances. We've been trying to think of a way to stop it without actually getting into open confrontation with the heavies. Obviously, we didn't have your imagination or, fair play to you, your bottle. We'll gladly help. We know the minute these guys hit the scheme. We'll set up a system of messengers that'll have you on them within ten minutes. These guys are getting as predictable as the insurance man or the paper boy. And they're starting to feel as respectable, getting righteous about looking after the poor junkies. They need a kick in the arse. I believe a horse has a very good kick.'

'How soon could you be ready, Billy?' Tom enquired.

'I'll call a meeting, tomorrow night. It'd be as soon as we can organise that. We'll take your idea and fit it in with what we know. I think that for the first few days it'll be easy enough on account of their predictability. Once they get wide to what you're at it might be more tricky, we'll see.'

'Thursday, dole day, is their busy day, that's four days from now. We'll try and be ready by then.'

'Okay,' Tom said, 'that'll be great.'

'I'll call down to you Wednesday morning and fill you in,' Billy promised.

'Thanks a lot,' Tom said.

'Shit, Tom, no matter what happens it'll be a bit of crack for us,' Billy chuckled. 'If it works, all the better.'

Tom spent the next few days with Joe. They discussed

which mount would be best suited for the new line of work. Weight was what they concluded would be the best qualification, the best thing, weight and size. The biggest hairy mare was chosen. She was ridden a lot over the next few days as Tom tried to turn her into something of a cattle pony. She was slow, but she was willing. She certainly preferred being ridden to pulling a laden cart. Tom avoided Marie's place, unsure of her feelings on the matter. On Tuesday evening, however, she sought him out. She found him in the garden.

'You were staying away,' she said flatly.

'I thought maybe that's what you wanted,' he answered.

'I was a bit confused the last time,' she explained. 'It shocked me to realise you might be capable of such violence, wondering would it ever turn on me or Tommy. Then after thinking about it a bit I realised I just wasn't trusting you. Surely I knew what you were capable of. I mean, why the hell were you in prison? And now, when your anger is very justified, none of it is aimed at me. Will you please forgive me?'

'It's alright,' Tom assured her, 'I'm not used to being around women much. Maybe there's just some things I should keep to myself.'

'Here we are, with a ten year old son and we know so little,' she offered, 'so little about each other, so little about feelings. When we made Tommy we were just children, and it seems to be taking us a while to grow up.'

'It's funny,' Tom remembered, 'my mother was talking about something like that recently, that it's better to be learning along with your children. To share the innocence.'

'Let's keep getting to know each other, right?' she suggested.

'Yes, please,' Tom said, taking her into his arms and holding her. 'Yes, please.'

Billy found him in the same garden the following morning. He greeted Tom excitedly. 'The Committee is delighted. We were up half the night working out the details. They are getting a real kick out of the whole idea. Half the time we spent arguing with the geniuses on the committee coming up with wild improvements on your plan. Anyhow, here's what we came up with. We figured there's no way to cover the whole scheme, that it's a horse you have, not a bleeding helicopter. So we picked an area with a lot of junkies that's easy to get around. Between Kylemore and Le Fanu was the bit we picked. If you are by the Tesco then you can get to any of the streets within minutes by using the connecting lanes. We have a load of young fellas as runners ready on each street. As soon as they cop a dealer, with one of them at every lane, they can actually pass the message to you from one to the next. You'll be directed at each point. No problem.' Billy finished, beaming.

'If two dealers turn up at the same time, then what?' Tom asked.

'Then it's up to you,' Billy told him. 'Wave one off and carry on with the other. It's unlikely. They all have different times for some reason.'

'There's one thing — ' Tom insisted, 'any trouble, like if one of them decides to put up a fight, I take care of it. I don't want anyone else hurt, right?'

'Okay.' Billy agreed. 'Nine in the morning we'll meet at the library and I'll let you meet the two lads who'll be nearest you so you'll know who to watch for the signal.'

'Magic!' Tom said. 'If everything goes okay then I'll have smack and money. I was planning to destroy the smack, but I just thought of the poor bastards waiting for it. What do you think?'

'Destroy it — definitely,' Billy emphasised. 'They'll go elsewhere for it. That should cause more confusion. A bunch of them turning up somewhere else will put some other bastard under pressure. It'll all help to highlight the situation. I mean you want the Cur embarrassed as soon as possible.'

'Right!' Tom agreed. 'The money then, your committee must have some kind of fund. Will they accept the money?'

'Gladly,' Billy said. 'We've a few families whose husbands or sons, or even mothers or daughters got fucked by smack that need help. It'd be only justice if smack was to provide that help. Aw, yeah, we'll gladly take it.'

'The area we're covering tomorrow, how many days can we knock out of it?' Tom enquired.

'We thought about that,' Billy told him. 'No more than three. Saturday should see them wide to it. So, two or three other areas are being looked into. People from those areas are setting it up like this one. They'll be on to me tomorrow night with what they've got. With a bit of luck we'll tackle another section Sunday or Monday.'

'Fair play to you, Billy, you thought of everything,' Tom congratulated him.

'Let's see what happens tomorrow before we get too cocky,' Billy admonished. 'I will say this, though, this is all very exciting. It'll be great for the young lads, an enterprise course in intelligence and strategy,' he finished, laughing.

'Till tomorrow then,' Tom said, and they shook hands before parting.

Chapter 19

Spike Richards had four calls behind him when he turned into the Drive. He was grumbling to himself about that bitch on Kylemore. Access to a steady supply for himself had numbed his sympathy to those less fortunate than himself.

'Snivelling cow,' he muttered. 'What right has she got being a junky. Whinging to me about her three kids. Thinks I'm the bleeding Vincent de Paul.'

The Spike maintained his own habit by dealing. His habit was his religion, his displaced Catholicism. He was now a self-righteous zealot. The 'snivelling cow's' offer of sexual favours in return for a tenner's worth of gear had offended his sense of the purity of his relationship with smack. Besides, it was bad business. A tenner lost to the altar of his addiction. Engrossed as he was in his litany, he almost failed to notice the rapidly approaching sound of horseshoes striking concrete. The clatter penetrated his unconscious mind but was quickly shrugged off as 'Another of those glue-sniffing cowboys that are always riding around this godforsaken kip'. His conscious mind was already slipping off on the tangent of how this glue-sniffing, being so cheap, was robbing honest dealers of potential custom. The shops should be stopped from selling it. His instincts dragged his eyes up from their smack-induced vacation and he froze. His mouth dropped open as he saw barrelling towards him the angel of death in the guise of an Apache, riding a huge piebald, swinging a warclub that looked exactly like a hurley stick. The huge animal met him chest-to-chest. His face was slammed by the muscular neck. As he flew, breathless, back against the railings, a passing iron-shod hoof smacked the back of his leg. He found himself sitting gasping on the pavement, watching the horse skidding around, sparks flying as iron scraped concrete, and walking back towards him. The huge head settled inches above his own, offering him a frightening view of poisonous-looking yellow teeth big enough to crunch his whole head.

'Take off your jacket and throw it on the deck.' The voice seemed to come from the sky. His moment's hesitation was prompted, not by an unco-operative motive, but by the sheer unreality of the situation. The stinging blow the flat of the hurley dealt his right ear removed any doubt that this was definitely happening. He struggled with his jacket, hypnotised all the while by the saliva dripping, as if in antici-pation of a feed, from those ghastly teeth.

'Now turn out your pockets,' the voice told him. 'I want to see the lining.' The Spike complied with fervour, money and keys spreading on the ground.

'Over on your belly and empty your back pockets,' he was ordered.

As the dealer did this, Tom hooked the jacket with the hurley stick and searched the pockets.

'Where's the smack?' Tom demanded.

'What sma . . . ? ' The blow from the hurley finished his half-hearted protestation of innocence. His arm became as numb as his leg.

'Here, here,' the Spike said quickly, reaching down his pants, producing a supermarket bag.

'Drop your strides,' he was ordered.

As he did, the sight of another bag earned him another vicious clatter of the hurley, this time to the other ear.

'That's it. That's all,' the dealer assured him, his fear convincing Tom. Tom threw him his jacket saying, 'Get out of here, next time you come around I'll break your fucking legs.'

The Spike nodded feverishly and scurried away dragging his dead leg, cathedral bells ringing in his ears. Penniless he wondered how he was going to get his own supply, the anguish of his sudden withdrawal overwhelming the pain of his battered body.

Tom dismounted, aware for the first time of the crowd. A young boy took the reins, his face beaming with admiration.

'Thanks,' Tom said and surveyed the crowd, absently rolling a cigarette. At almost every door at least one woman stood, whole families in some cases. On the street, young and not-so-young men stood silently, many with brushes, hammers, tyre levers in their hands, the innocent weapons of the household. A teenage boy, one of the boys Billy Ryan had introduced him to, calmly gathered the items left by the dealer.

'There's a nice strong cup of tea for you son.' An old woman handed him a cup of tea. 'It's a grand thing you're doing,' she thanked him and walked away.

As the silence ebbed and the excited conversations grew, Billy pushed through the crowd.

'They're already talking about this on the next street. It'll hit the shops in a few minutes. It went alright?' he asked.

'Perfect' Tom told him. 'There's the stuff.'

The boy handed the money and the bags to Billy. He transferred the money and belongings into one bag, having spilled the heroin into a pile on the ground.

'What do we do with it, Tom?' he wondered aloud.

'Burn it,' Tom suggested.

A man in the crowd said he had a gallon of petrol in the car. Billy took it from him and saturated the pile.

'You light it, Tom,' he said.

Tom struck a match and dropped it on the petrol-soaked heroin. As the flames leapt up the people let out a powerful cheer.

Chapter 20

Tom and Billy walked back to the place they had selected as the central point. Before they reached it a teenage girl ran to them. 'There's another one already doing business at the playground,' she told them excitedly.

The playground was fairly close. He could see it from where he was. This time he was exiting from a crowded stage. There were quite a lot of people around by now aware of what he was up to. Tom couldn't resist a little showmanship. He whacked the horse into the closest she could manage to a canter before leaping aloft. Most of his audience were women, but the oohs and aahs were inaudible to him. Billy and a few young lads gave him a little face with their yahoos.

Cantering towards the playground he soon realized this one was not going to be as simple as the first time. This was no distracted guy walking alone in an empty street. What he was approaching was a crowd of mostly young men and women. There appeared to be an argument going on, all present seemingly involved. There was no way to distinguish which of them was the dealer. Tom's snooker-playing guided his move. Split the reds.

Eighty feet from them he raised the hurley and yelled as loudly and threateningly as he could, urging top speed from the lumbering mare. For two seconds he thought he had failed. They stood staring at his approach. Then one ran. In a split second the group exploded apart in as many different directions as there were people. One remained, stuffing a bag into his leather jacket. He poised, awaiting the charge. Tom quickly realised what he was up against. This was no dopehead stunned into a panicked immobility. This guy had sized the situation. He was going to defend his pitch. The guy stood like a goalie before a penalty shot. Left or right? Admiring his moves Tom realised that the dealer was not going to avoid the hurley as a less-confident man would. He intended to come in under the swing. Tom maintained the feint until the last second, and, sure the guy was committed to his move, he spun the stick so the club end rested against his stomach, blade edge forward, guessing instinctively the height. The hurley connected with the bridge of the man's nose, the momentum of horse and rider pushing against the man's upward surge to press it slightly downwards. Blood rushed down the man's throat and he gagged, stumbling backwards, his nose broken. The horse was coming to a halt, animal and man moving in the same direction, at almost the same speed. Tom had the leisure to aim his second swing. He chose the shins, using the edge of the stick again. The man was crippled for the moment.

Tom addressed him, 'Do I finish it or do you co-operate?'

On the ground the man considered him. 'Who the fuck are you?'

'My name is Tom Reid,' Tom told him.

Rubbing his agonised shins, the dealer said, 'My older brother was in the Joy same time as you. I don't want any hassle with you myself, but you know this won't stop here, you fucking know that. What the hell are you playing at?'

'First, I want the smack and the money,' Tom said.

The dealer produced the bag from his jacket, and money from his various pockets. He put the money in the bag with the drugs and handed it to Tom. 'Okay,' Tom nodded his approval, 'the Cur has something of mine and I'm getting it back.'

'My brother told me you weren't a guy to fuck about with,' the man admitted, 'but remember the Cur can afford a lot of help.'

'You don't deal around here again,' Tom warned him.

'Fine with me,' the man shrugged. 'There'll just be someone else.'

Just then a motor-bike skidded to a halt by the fallen man. The rider appraised the situation. 'What the fuck?' he addressed the dealer, eyeing Tom all the while with aggression.

'Cool it,' the dealer snapped, pulling himself up on the back

of the bike. Mounted, he said, 'I'll tell my brother I saw yeh.'
'Go!' he told the driver.

When the bike tried to leave Tom saw a crowd of perhaps fifty men surround the scene of the action, all holding a weapon of some kind, their silence an effective measure of their intended menace.

'Let them through.' Tom spoke with authority, and the crowd sullenly parted, the bike speeding through the gap.

The man with the petrol appeared beside Tom, shaking the can. Tom threw the bag to Billy Ryan who separated the money, emptying the packets of white powder on the ground. Again they burned the smack.

Walking back to their waiting area, Tom commented to Billy, 'That's a dangerous-looking crowd, getting bigger all the time.'

'They're pissed off with this business too long, worrying about their kids or their brothers and sisters. This is the first time they've had a chance to have a real go at it.'

'Jesus, Billy, I'm getting scared they might lynch somebody,' Tom voiced his concern.

'You seem to have them in the palm of your hand,' Billy noted.

'So far,' Tom mused.

Tom's next assignment almost stumped him. Later in the afternoon he was directed to Kylemore Avenue. His target turned out to be a pretty girl of about eighteen. Having smacked her on the arse a few times with the hurley, he finally backed her up against a garden wall. His demand for the drugs and the money was met with a flirtatious 'Why don't you get down and get it yourself, cowboy?' The slap was so sudden, the mare almost reared. A large woman, still wearing her apron had the girl by the hair. She slapped her viciously. 'I'll get it for you, son,' she told him confidently. She did, planting a sound kick on the girl's exquisite backside, expediting her departure. The woman performed the burning of the smack.

'Treat them the same as the men,' she told him. 'A bitch just like that one got my fifteen-year-old son hooked. He's in jail now and I never thought I'd say it, but I'm glad. He ended up dealing to kids younger than himself. I pray now that he'll just get off the stuff in there.'

Chapter 21

At seven that evening Tom gave up for the day. No more dealers had been spotted in the area. A young boy took the mare home for him and he went for a pint with Billy. Their entrance was greeted with cheers and congratulations. Billy counted the money. There was nearly four hundred pounds.

'One of the lads there today who used to do a bit of smack himself reckoned we burned about fifteen hundred quid's worth of smack,' Billy told him.

'Do you think we'll get anybody tomorrow, they might figure it's just too hot for them.' Tom asked.

'I'd say so. Today I reckon a few slipped by us. They'll still think they can tomorrow. Don't forget that the dealers who are strung out themselves have their habits to support. The ones in it for profit stand to lose over a ton a day. Somebody will turn up.'

Tom had dinner with Marie that evening. His day's work was already legend. Young Tommy's excited account of the day's happenings rang with embellishment. To him it was the big picture with his daddy playing John Wayne. Naturally his confrontation with the woman played a little part in Tommy's scenario. That was like the kissing scene, a yawn interrupting the action.

'A smack on the arse,' his summation of the incident.

'The smack on the arse didn't work,' he admitted, allowing the boy a few seconds for the significance of that confession to sink in. 'She just smiled up at me, putting it to me. If you want what I got . . . take it.'

To his left Marie suddenly laughed, much to Tommy's consternation, as he looked from one parent to the other.

Tom continued. 'So what am I supposed to do, give her a

smack across the head with the hurley, get down off the horse, give her a few clatters, then rip her clothes apart to get what I want. If you must picture the scene, picture that.'

The boy did.

'I would have thought a smack on the arse and a big horse coming at her would have scared her, but it didn't. She didn't panic they way we think women are supposed to. She was brave, brave enough to keep a clear head and size up the situation. Then she fought back with the weapons she had, woman's weapons. She disarmed me. I lost. And, in that second, I realised I could lose the whole goddamn war. All they have to do is send women.'

'But the other two?' Tommy insisted. 'What about them?'

'Okay,' Tom said, 'the first guy was easy, the mare had him scared shitless. With the second guy I was lucky, the first move worked. If it hadn't, the both of us would have been on the ground and there would be two very sore men this evening instead of just one. But let's get back to the other thing. If Missus Tierney hadn't stepped in and saved my face, today would not have been as successful as it was. I set out today to stop a few dealers from doing business and I did. Tomorrow I will try and do the same, only tomorrow I'll go out there a little wiser, or maybe just not as stupid.'

Tommy finished his dinner in silence. Later, as he was about to go out, Tom stopped him, saying, 'After today some people are going to be very pissed off with me, so while you're out be careful. If you're going someplace let us know beforehand. Understand?'

The boy nodded and left.

'Tom, I only thought of that as you were saying it.' Marie said. 'Could it happen?'

'It's something he's better expecting. I don't think anything will happen this soon. Tommy's pretty wide,' he reassured her.

'Tom, when I think about it, it makes me worry,' Marie admitted.

'The minute I feel there's the slightest chance of that we'll get him offside. Try not to think of it any more than you have to.'

'That's easy to say,' she said, with a touch of bitterness.

'Marie,' there was a demand in his tone, 'we can't turn the clock back. It happened. You have to let your common sense rule your emotions. Be careful. Keep your eyes open, but you have to go on living.'

'I know,' she said resignedly, 'I know.'

Silence fell between them for a while, a not uncomfortable silence. Each following their own thoughts, Tom voiced his eventually. 'I've been looking at women all my life. I suppose that's all I've been doing, looking at them. In the last few weeks I've really had to see them. My mother, when I got out, your lovely self, now those two women today.' He laughed. 'I wish I'd stuck to the horses, they're so much easier. That woman dealer today, so pretty, so sure of herself. It was hard not to forget the dirty game she was in. The woman who hit her, tougher than a lot of men I know. And the people, the crowd gets bigger every time. They look so dangerous, they even scare me. But today I'd have ended up looking like an eejit without them. I suppose it is going according to the plan, but only because all the things I didn't expect are working for me.'

'Don't knock it,' Marie said reverently.

'Amen,' Tom replied.

Chapter 22

The place where Tom had kept vigil was milling with people. It was Saturday morning. The huge supermarket nearby was doing a mighty business. Chosen for the number of ways away from it, the hub, it had the same number to it. The supermarket, like an anthill in reverse, drew in thousands empty-handed and spewed them out laden. Besides shoppers, many people, men, women and children, hung about waiting for whatever excitement was coming. The boys Tom had been introduced to that morning as his closest lookouts, were sometimes lost from his sight in the crowd. Even the placid mare betrayed a little uneasiness at the constant hubbub.

The signal, when it came, he almost missed. From the corner of his eye he caught the waving figure perched above the crowd, hanging from the tall railings that backed Kylemore Drive. Tom mounted the mare and turned her towards the waving boy. The crowd, as if aware of the signal, parted. Cantering the mare proved a lot less difficult than he'd imagined. He was passed from one pointing boy to another until he saw his prey. He was barely aware of the crowd dashing behind him, concentrating as he was on the stooped figure of a man, a hundred yards ahead, who, thank fuck, had his back to him. Tom kicked into the mare's trundling gallop, the approaching clatter bringing the man around. Seeing the hurley-wielding rider approach, the man simply raised both arms high above his head in a universal gesture of surrender. Tom reined in the mare beside him. He was a gaunt, prematurely grey-haired, middle-aged man. With Tom above him, he began to empty his pockets of money and several dozen cellophane packets of white powder.

He spoke hesitantly, 'I heard about you. I was hoping to

miss you. I'd be very grateful if you didn't use that,' he nodded at the hurley stick. 'I'm not that well,' he added.

'Why are you doing this?' Tom asked him.

'I've got the bad habit myself,' was his plaintive reply.

At that a young girl of perhaps thirteen ran from the larger-than-ever crowd of which Tom had just become aware. The girl rushed towards the man and threw her arms around his waist protectively.

'Leave him alone, Mister' she pleaded, yet there was a demand in her plea as if she would fight if necessary. Tom knew she would.

'My Da is very sick,' she explained without shame, head up.

'Take him home,' Tom said softly, but added, 'He'll get hurt if he comes again.'

She led the man towards a rapidly-parting crowd. Some gently touched the girl as she passed.

A boy took the money, while another burned the smack. There was little joy in the silent crowd. Tom dismounted and accepted a cigarette from a man nearby. Walking back, considerately left alone, Tom remembered the Cur. In all the immediacy of the previous day he hadn't been thinking about him. How far away the days of the planning of this campaign. How whimsical now seemed his anger for his beautiful stallion. Set beside the evil smack, the theft of the horse, with all its malicious intent, seemed as nothing. A cold white anger settled indigestibly in the base of his stomach.

Chapter 23

Back at his post Tom simmered, but the amount of time he spent waiting for his next victim was enough to cool his anger. He was pleased with this, as he figured he was more efficient operating coldly. Two more dealers fell to him that Saturday, both men, and handled with relative ease. Tom considered it another successful day.

Again, one of the boys took the mare back to the house for him, and he joined Billy for a drink. They spoke for a while about the events of the day, lingering on the incident of the young girl. Her simple courage had moved them both greatly. Billy vowed his commitment. He would strive to help the father, try and get him on a treatment programme. Finally Billy asked, 'You know the Tosh Hennessy?'

'Aye,' Tom replied. 'The coalman who lives on Decies.'

'Yeah,' Billy said. 'He approached the Decies Committee last night offering his services. He feels he could do what you're doing in the lower end of the scheme. He has the horses and he's certainly tough enough. I think myself he is responsible enough. With two of you at it, and we have plenty of people for backup, we'd be more than twice as effective. What do you think?'

Tom whistled softly in amazement. 'Jesus, this is really getting bigger than I'd ever imagined.' He paused, thinking. 'It seems like a good idea. As you said, it will be twice as effective. It will also give the impression of a popular movement which from my original point of view, will certainly reflect badly on the Cur. Mind you, Billy, my original motive seems pretty silly now, especially after today. That father and daughter scene really brought home to me the horrors of the smack scene. Yeh, I know the Tosh really well. He'll be able to handle it fine. We'll leave off till Monday, but we should have a meeting tomorrow. I'd especially like to talk to the Tosh. Fill him in on what I've learned from the last three days.'

Sunday it made the papers, at least a paragraph in each one, front page of the *Sunday World*. 'Lone Ranger Rides Again' was the headline. 'The bareback conscience of Ballyfermot rides roughshod over drugs operation. Sources in Ballyfermot . . . Police – no comment.' Tom guessed someone had phoned it in.

At lunchtime Tom and Joe were in the County Bar. A well-dressed, middle-aged man approached their table. 'Tom Reid?' he enquired.

Tom nodded.

'My name is Robbie Simpson. I write for the *Sunday World*. May I join ye?'

With their permission, the reporter sat down.

'Are you the one my paper euphemistically called "The Lone Ranger"?' he asked Tom.

'There was no photograph, but I imagine it was me alright,' Tom confessed.

'Do you want to tell me what's going on?' he asked.

'I don't know.' Tom said. 'I'm not sure at this stage whether any more publicity would be helpful or not. The police haven't got involved so far, and for a while I'd prefer it that way. Another week without them would be grand.'

'From me you'd get a week. Our next edition won't hit the presses until Saturday,' the reporter informed them. 'I'd like background and a week around you, if that's possible. You'd be well paid,' he added.

'How well?' Tom enquired.

'Five hundred' was the reply.

'You give a grand to the Parents Committee and I'll give you what you want, Tom gambled.

The reporter laughed and offered Tom his hand. They shook on it. The reporter ordered drinks for them all and laid a tape recorder on the table in front of Tom.

'Okay,' he began, 'what's going on?'

'You've heard of the Cur McMurragh?' Tom asked the reporter, observed his acknowledgement, and continued. 'I'm going to put him out of business.'

'Why pick him?'

'He stole my horse,' Tom replied.

Simpson laughed. 'Are you serious?'

Tom explained, bringing the story up to date, including the Tosh's recruitment. 'As from Monday the Lone Ranger will have a Tonto, or should I say Tonto will have a Lone Ranger.'

'This is absolutely fantastic,' the reporter exclaimed, 'and I use the word "fantastic" advisedly.'

'As I already said, so far the cops haven't been around. We've only been at this for two days. If we can knock another three or four days out of it, enough attention should be focussed on the Cur to put him in the shit with the Board. Then it should be his move. What do you think?' Tom finished with the question.

'I don't know,' Simpson answered, 'but I sure want to be around to find out. Also, my presence may just afford you a little protection if things get rough.'

They talked some more and the reporter left, agreeing to meet Tom the following morning.

That afternoon Tom met with the Committee. Now they had twice the arrangements to make. Two separate networks of spies, two of runners and sentries. There were volunteers aplenty. Those with the experience of the previous week paired off with their newly-elected opposite numbers to impart the knowledge, most importantly, what they'd learned from their mistakes. Tom's opposite number, the Tosh, was an enormous man, at six one, weighing eighteen stone. That twenty years of lugging bags of coal had hardened the muscles. Tom spent the best part of an hour giving him the benefit of his learned experience. The Tosh was a quiet, intelligent man, whose fifteen-year-old son was undergoing treatment to cure his heroin addiction. Tom was confident that the man would not allow this fact to affect his judgement.

'Getting into the papers and all, so public, makes me scared,' Marie confided in Tom that evening. 'I'm glad there was no picture, or your name.'

'From here on,' Tom told her simply, 'I'll have a reporter with me all the time.'

'How soon before we get a comeback?' she asked, worried.

'I don't know,' Tom admitted. 'Tomorrow there'll be

another just like me on the street. Tosh Hennessy, you know him, don't you?'

'Sure,' Marie said.

'He's volunteered to tackle the lower end of the scheme. That will speed things up. We'll get some reaction sooner, twice as many dealers, twice as much trouble and expense for them. Surely the Cur will get some stick then,' Tom explained.

'That might bring it to a head alright.' Marie hoped.

'I think everything will be okay for the next few days. Up till now it's been just me. After tomorrow they'll know we're not going to go away, that it's getting bigger. They'll have to change tactics in some way.'

Tom's quota of victims for Monday was two. He was being avoided. Tosh, on the other hand, unexpectedly, dealt easily with four. His phenomenal strength and his colossal horse made fleas of the pedestrian dealers. He picked one victim easily from the ground and shook co-operation from him. On Tuesday only two dealers were intercepted. The Committee confidently reported those two as all that had braved the area. Known addicts from the scheme were observed taking the bus into town, presumably to find an alternative source of supply. This development did not displease Tom, as it meant the Cur's business was being picked up by his competitors. The raising of the city dealers' profile by the sudden increase in the number of anxious junkies led to an increase of busts by the city drug squad. On Wednesday afternoon Billy approached Tom on the run, extremely excited. 'It's happening all over, Tom,' he shouted, 'Jesus Christ, it's happening all over the city.'

Before Tom could ask what, Billy continued, 'We're getting reports from Crumlin, Cabra, Ballymun, Dun Laoghaire, everywhere. There's guys doing it everywhere. Lone fucking Rangers all over the place. This is it. The fat's really hit the fire now.'

'Get your breath, Billy,' Tom said. 'Then tell me, slowly.'

Billy produced cigarettes and used the time it took to get them both lit to calm himself. 'There's guys on horses all over the city doing exactly what we're doing. They're taking out dealers by the bleeding score. We're hitting them all over the city now. This is fantastic. The same reaction everywhere. The people are all behind it. They're determined and they're feeling their own power. They're getting results.'

Billy became silent as his mind devoured the whole picture. The same picture played in the theatre of Tom's imagination. Tom, however, was already anticipating the result. Citywide, as it was becoming, it was moving the game out of the sole province of the Cur, and into the arena of the Board. The Cur must be seen as the cause of the crisis. The Board must be made to understand that all this aggravation derived directly from the Cur's paranoia, his inability to distinguish business from personal revenge. Up to now the Cur's business alone was being hurt. This new development would be affecting every member of the Board. Again, Tom's clever plan was making waves where he had expected ripples, a goddamn hurricane where he'd been fanning a breeze.

'Billy, listen to me,' Tom shook his friend from his smiling reverie. 'This is going to change everything. We're not just hurting the Cur, we're getting at every supplier in the city now. Work out the kind of money it must be costing them, let alone the loss of face. They won't just lie down for that. Things are going to happen and we're going to have to try and figure out what.'

'Like what?' Billy asked.

'I'm not sure,' Tom admitted, 'but their whole set-up depends on widespread distribution. We've already seen what happens if the addicts from just Ballyer head for town to score. It makes the city dealers too obvious. They start being busted. Imagine junkies from all the schemes freaking out for a fix, there'll be chaos. The suppliers have to keep their present network. Think about it, using the horses we've been able to overcome the dealers fairly easily and mostly without violence. Dealers sending in some muscle now won't work because of the crowds. And those crowds are pretty angry. They'd love an excuse to lash out. Jesus, last week, I was shitting in case they would.'

'What can they do, then?' Billy wondered.

'The ice-cream van,' was Tom's reply.

Some enterprising dealers had come upon the brilliant idea of using ice-cream vans as a cover for their business. That innocent bell-ringing set-up was devilishly clever. They even made money selling ice-cream. Junkies love ice-cream, especially when the bottom of their cone contained a little surprise. Nothing looked more innocent than people to-ing and fro-ing between house and van, money passing hands an expected part of the transaction. The bell-ringing, a perfect signal.

'There's not enough vans in the city,' Billy pointed out.

'The insurance man, the check man, the vegetable man, even the coalman,' Tom listed. 'The point I'm making is cars and vans. Eight horses at least, pulling every one. Any hassle and they just take off.'

'I see,' Billy said. 'How do we handle that?'

'The spud, Billy, the good old potato' Tom laughed.

Chapter 24

On Friday the first of the cars arrived. The first transaction betrayed them. Expected as they were, the Committee had decided on the strategy of watching the known users, thus identifying which of the many stopping cars was the one they wanted. In the car were two men. They had no intention of getting out at the house of their customer. They blew the horn and waited. A young man left the house, approached the car, got his dope, paid his money and rushed back into the house. Then the motor died and repeated attempts to start it again failed. An ominous silent crowd appeared as if from nowhere, and simply stood watching the car. The two men pressed the buttons on both sides, locking their doors, and the horseman approached. He rode up to the front of the car at a canter and struck the windscreen with a steel-banded hurley. The glass didn't break, but formed an opaque cobweb, blinding their forward vision. The horseman brought his mount around and tapped politely at the window on the driver's side. Using the stick as a pointer he indicated that they should look behind. They did, and saw a man carefully lowering an old necktie into the petrol tank, first one end and then the other, making sure it was completely soaked with petrol. Waving a cigarette lighter he looked at the horseman as if awaiting a signal. Tom, from the horse, said just loud enough for the driver to hear, 'Will you get out now, or when it's burning?'

They got out and stood by the car.

'You know what I want. Whether you get hurt or not is up to you,' he told them quietly.

They began to empty their pockets, putting the money and smack on the bonnet.

Satisfied they'd gotten everything, the crowd parted and

allowed the two men through. Once past the crowd, the men took off at a run, to the accompaniment of a great burst of laughter and cheering. A young boy removed the potato from the exhaust pipe of the car and looked at it, astonished at its power. He'd put it there on instructions when the occupants of the car were transacting with the junkie and the dope. He had never seen the trick work before. He knew now that it did.

Tom wondered how many poor motorists in the neighbourhood were going to curse him for that bit of education when this trouble was over.

The car was searched and another stash of smack was found, much bigger than the one carried by the dealer. As the smack was being destroyed, a large van arrived and parked by the car. Three young men got out and Tom told them to 'go ahead'. Taking tools and a garage jack from the van they began to remove every saleable item from the car. Forty minutes later all that remained of the car was the empty shell of the body. It had been a two-year-old car worth four thousand pounds. This was getting damned expensive for the drug industry.

The potato was not the only weapon at the disposal of Tom and the Committee. There were certain characteristics of the streets of Ballyfermot, indeed the streets of most of the Corporation housing schemes, that were used in the guerilla war against the dealers.

Joy-riding had reached epidemic proportions. People's lives were being seriously endangered. Injury and death became an eventuality, became a fact. The people were again forced to act. They reasoned that by closing the streets it would confine these activities to the main roads, which they could not close. Concrete pillars were erected at one end of most streets, creating cul-de-sacs through which the speeding cars could not go. Drivers living in these streets now had the minor inconvenience of having to turn their cars and leave the streets as they'd entered. A small price to pay for the safety of themselves and their children. These cul-de-sacs became natural traps for the cars of the dealers. Once one entered a street, a truck across the entrance or a few oil drums full of stones rolled into place meant they could not drive out.

Tom's second car had decided the barrels could be moved by a fast car, probably thinking them empty, a bluff. The two men were the first casualties of the campaign. Dazed and bleeding from split heads they were relieved of their possessions and their car was also systematically stripped. They'd succeeded in shifting the barrels seven feet.

That evening the shells of seven such cars littered Ballyfermot. By Saturday morning, they were on the back of a truck heading for Hammond Lane Foundry. That Friday night, however, Tom and Billy wondered over a drink at the conspicuous absence of the police.

'Everyone else in Ballyer knew what was going on. Where the fuck were they?' Billy said to the company in general.

'One explanation is that they are staying away,' Tom offered.

At that the reporter entered. He'd been coming and going for the week.

'Ye had a good day, lads,' he congratulated. 'Citywide, my sources estimate around fifty cars. A few injuries, nothing serious, a dead horse in Finglas, got in the way of a fleeing car. It stopped the car. The driver was damned near beaten to death.'

'Today will never happen again,' Tom said, with great seriousness. 'They'll never let that happen again. From here on in it will be all-out war. They lost too much today. My guess is there'll be a big meeting tonight or tomorrow, and the next time, tomorrow, Sunday or Monday, they'll come gunning. From here on in, we'd better be prepared to retreat, vanish. Billy, get the word around and I mean everywhere, from now on be very careful.'

The men discussed the strategy for a while until Tom, satisfied with the precautions, caught the reporter's eye and led him to a quiet corner.

'How's your story coming?' he asked him.

'There's still tomorrow, whatever might happen then,' the reporter told him.

'I don't think anything will, but we'll be prepared anyway,' Tom replied.

'Whatever does happen, last week's developments will guarantee the front page. That's already settled. There's something else on your mind, isn't there?'

'Sure is,' Tom paused again, rolling a cigarette, composing

his thoughts. He went on, 'I still want that son-of-a-bitch, and I want my stallion, understand?'

'What do you think I can do?' the reporter asked.

Tom told him. 'I want the Board to know that this is all happening because the Cur abused his position on that Board. I realise you can't exactly print that. I also realise you can't even print the Cur's name, but is there some way you can phrase it so the message will be obvious to those concerned?'

'Probably,' the reporter replied, 'but there are several reasons why that might not be advisable for you or for the parents' committees. It will look a lot better for them if this movement seems like a spontaneous, popular reaction to the heroin problem. They'll get a lot more support and sympathy for what was, after all, a series of illegal acts. From your point of view, it would make you a target personally for any retaliation.'

The reporter got up at that and strolled up to the bar, leaving Tom to chew on what he'd said so far. He returned some minutes later.

'Tom,' he said, sipping his whiskey, 'I'm one of the best reporters in the country. One of the reasons I am is that not only do I know a lot of important people, but I also have the ear of those people. One of them is the chairman of that Board you so casually refer to. I see him tonight. I tell him exactly what happened here and why. You then become the instigator of all this trouble. Do you want to be the scapegoat, pardon the pun, just for a horse?'

Tom answered simply: 'Yes.'

Chapter 25

Marie was at his mother's house. Her nervousness was apparent.

'I heard what went down today Tom, I'm scared,' she gripped his hand.

'I'll get you and Tommy away,' Tom reassured her.

'And you, will you run and hide?' she pleaded.

'You know I can't,' he told her. 'A week ago I'd never have believed today could have happened. I'm getting close.'

'Close to getting killed,' she said angrily.

'Not if I can help it,' Tom answered, and pulled her close. He stroked her hair back from her flushed face.

'Tomorrow you and Tommy are going West. For your safety and mine. My not getting killed now depends on concentrating only on the things going on around me. I have to be sure you two are safely out of it, love. I've no intention of getting killed, but this thing can't be stopped. It has to be finished.'

In Tom's arms Marie nodded and cried softly. She understood. She would accept whatever he decided, but he was in the thick of it, she powerless on the sidelines. Now of necessity she must move far away, deprived of the little comfort of at least knowing the outcome immediately, be it good or bad.

'I feel like such a ninny, Tom,' she sobbed. 'I knew it must come to this. I just had no idea of what it would feel like. I didn't know what it was like to have a man to lose. Don't let me lose you, Tom, please.'

Tom's voice carried his emotion. 'This is a new time for both of us, love. I didn't know what it was like to have a woman to lose. But I do know having each other doesn't shut the rest of the world out. I came into the comfort of your world with all the problems of mine. That's all we have to build on. We can't pretend it's any other way. We have to love each other, not just for what we are, but for what we bring to each other.'

Then, as if to make a liar of himself, Tom held her so tightly that not a hint of the world could squeeze between them. They stood in the embrace until they became stiff and uncomfortable.

Tom spoke, 'Do you understand love, that we can't be like this all the time. We have a boy to feed and clothe and prepare for life. We have to live our separate lives to do that. But I do hope we'll share those lives as much as possible.'

Marie pushed him away to arm's length, looked into his face awhile before she kissed him with an open and generous mouth.

'We'd better go and arrange my trip,' she said, and led him to the kitchen where the rest of the family were waiting.

Over dinner, the whole family together celebrated the success of the campaign. The men spoke loudly and laughed. The women smiled and hid their worries.

Chapter 26

That night Marie clung to Tom.

Joe arrived early in a borrowed car to take her and Tommy to the station. For the most part the parting was quiet. The adults had little to say. Tommy however was excited with anticipation of the trip west and disappointment at leaving what he saw as the war zone. He mixed these conflicting emotions easily, as only a child can.

The emptiness of the house surprised Tom as he sat finishing the pot of tea. An hour later he and his mare were at the spot chosen for that day's surveillance. Lookouts and runners were positioned. Several men from the Committee stood with him. They talked quietly. As was usual on Saturday morning, the streets were thronged with people. Many stopped to talk and express encouragement, some to make suggestions. Every one, it seemed, supported their actions. The hours passed pleasantly without the appearance of any suspicious cars or people. Word reached them that the Tosh at his station was meeting the same lack of activity. It was turning out as Tom had expected. The drug dealers were consolidating, gearing up for a later assault.

At four in the afternoon an unmarked police car stopped near Tom and his friends. A burly detective approached the crowd.

'Which of you is Tom Reid?' he demanded.

One of the men asked, 'Who wants to know?'

The detective produced his ID and again demanded that Tom Reid identify himself.

Tom stepped forward and stood before the man.

'You are to come with me to the station,' he told Tom.

'Is this an arrest?' Tom enquired quietly.

'If necessary,' the detective threatened.

Tom gave instructions to one of the men to return the mare to his house, and followed the cop to the car. They drove in silence to the garda station.

In the station Tom was led to a room in the back. Seated behind a desk was a uniformed superintendent. Standing against the wall was a very tough-looking man dressed in a short nylon jacket and jeans. The gun under his arm he made no effort to hide. The uniformed man, whom Tom guesed to be about sixty, stood and offered his hand.

'I'm Superintendent Foote. This is Inspector Burke of the Task Force.'

Tom accepted his hand and a firm handshake. The other man didn't move from his languid position against the wall.

'Mr. Reid,' the Super addressed Tom. 'We've been monitoring your activities for the past few weeks, and I must say I have been very impressed with your success. Your campaign has been admirably conducted and has escalated far more than we had at first anticipated. It would seem there is a groundswell of deep feeling about the problem of heroin. Citywide your people have cost the drug barons more expense in two weeks than the combined efforts of our agencies over a period of months. I offer my congratulations, Mr. Reid. However, we feel we have reached a point whereby we cannot see ourselves remaining on the sidelines any longer.'

He stopped speaking, looked at Tom, offering him the floor, should he choose to speak. Tom, from his experience with the police, chose silence.

As if the Super understood, he nodded and continued. 'As I understand, your motivation in this affair is rather simplistic,' he paused again, and seeing Tom still disinclined to comment, continued, 'the theft of your horse it seems.'

As Tom remained unwilling to speak, he lost a little of his patience. 'You do understand, Mr. Reid, the success of your campaign was due in no small measure to our choosing to allow your people to continue. We would have been, in fact should have been, obliged to halt your patently illegal activity.'

Tom spoke: 'In order to have stopped us, you would have needed as good a network as we had. This was an entirely different situation than the time the parents' committees were picketing the houses of known suppliers. That you could see, and when you decided you didn't like the people doing your job you could march in there and break a few heads. The heads of people, respectable people, who were trying to make their neighbourhoods safe for their children. People who were driven to that action by the inability of your agencies to do that very necessary job. This time, I doubt if you had enough manpower to police areas we didn't know we'd be in until minutes before we got there. That was only possible for us because we had the co-operation of practically every man, woman and child in the scheme. The kind of co-operation your past attitudes have made it impossible for you to get.'

'You seem to have a rather superior attitude for a coalman,' the Super spat at Tom.

'Fuck you too,' Tom replied pleasantly.

The Task Force detective moved quickly from the wall. Tom was almost sorry when the authoritative shout of the Super stopped him just two feet from him.

Tom smiled at the younger man, unable to resist taunting him.

The Super broke the tension. 'There is some truth in what you say, Mr. Reid. However, the dismantling of the cars was something we could easily have stopped. It was such a nice touch, I have to admit I enjoyed it. Still, this is getting us nowhere. What do you anticipate next?'

'We have no option but to continue our campaign,' Tom told him, 'but we have been stressing to our people that at the sight of a gun they must disappear. Up to that moment the strategy remains the same. Blocked in as we've had them, they'll be in a position where your bully boys could easily clean them up. You'd be getting them redhanded with smack and guns.'

'Excellent, Mr. Reid,' the Super acknowledged. 'It seems that I don't have to waste time explaining. Excuse my earlier remark. Now, our information from the inside suggests Tuesday as their day of action. On that day we'll be ready to pick up where you leave off.'

'Super,' Tom said, 'my experience with Dumbo Deegan gives me reason to worry about your security. Our people won't know about your involvement, yours do.'

'My dear man,' the policeman replied, 'the three of us are the only people who know of this at present. On Monday night the squads used will be briefed on a need-to-know basis. Believe me, Dumbo Deegan is in no way part of our plans. Satisfied?'

Tom conceded with a shrug.

The Super added: 'You can use the Rathmines incident as our reason for having you here. I presume you are capable of concocting a convincing story.'

The Super stood up and offered Tom his hand. 'Please accept my apology for my previous lack of tact. Until Tuesday then.'

Tom accepted his hand and thus his apology: 'I'll walk back to my friends. It will be more like the way you usually treat your suspects.'

He left the station thinking, 'The Cur's back is about to be broken.'

Chapter 27

The horsemen of the city maintained their vigilance for the rest of the weekend. The lack of activity surprised few, Tom least of all. They guessed in their heart of hearts that their enemy was regrouping, preparing for their next strategy. Every committee in every suburb warned its members of the possibility of the gun. Every committee repeatedly emphasised retreat at the first glimpse of a firearm. Thinkers among them puzzled at the absence of police, and realised also that the appearance of guns would push the battle out of the arena of their capabilities. They wracked their brains, seeking a strategy to meet that possible eventuality. No simple solution presented itself. The hand must simply be played out. Regrouping would then be the prerogative of the committees. In the meantime, vigilance.

Addicts from the suburbs flocked to town. Desperate, in large numbers, they frightened the city dealers undercover. The few dealers, equally desperate, who tried to cater to their needs, were easily busted. It was just too obvious, too frantic to be missed. The movement of heroin was at a standstill. Sadly, only the poor addict suffered. The rich had their exclusive suppliers, discreet, unnoticed in their respectability, their product of a far better quality than that of the street addict. Even among junkies class discrimination exists.

Tom leaned on his mare for two days. He rested, knowing nothing would happen until Tuesday. He chatted with whoever stopped, ate sandwiches, drank tea from a flask and waited. Success on Tuesday must bring him closer to the Cur. The stallion he put to one side, out of mind in the promised care of the Wren. Copies of the *Sunday World* had been circulating since Saturday evening. The reporter had done a great job. Governed by the laws of libel he could not name an alleged drug baron, but anyone involved in the business would recognise the Cur. Anyone with the power of thought could deduce that this citywide campaign had emanated from an inept petty action by this particular individual. Responsibility for this groundswell of reaction was left like an abandoned bastard on the doorstep of one whose judgement was impaired by the unwise abuse of his own products. Sections of the two-page article were written especially for the attention not only of the Board but also the entire underworld. The intention was a complete loss of face for the Cur, and through him the Board itself. Coupled with a successful day on Tuesday, this coverage must surely put the Cur in deep shit. Out on a limb, getting within Tom's reach. Martin's words echoed in Tom's head, 'slowly, deliberately and with pleasure'. The pleasure touched him now, tempered slightly by his natural instinct not to count his chickens. He did, however, smile at the cracks spreading rapidly across the eggs.

Chatting those days away, Tom was unusually good company. In such form, strangely, the absence of Marie and his son affected him more. He'd have loved to have shared his excitement with them, but common sense told him their safety and his necessary freedom of movement were best served by the present arrangement. He missed them badly. His reunion with Marie, his adult relationship with her, meant far more than he'd thought. Actually, it was the first time he'd had to think about it. Up to now it had been so immediate. It was all feelings and actions. Separated now, it was thought, memory and anticipation. They had finally become his family.

'Sounds serious, Tom,' Joe said, when he heard this confession. 'I love your timing, big brother. Your whole world threatening to blow up in your face, and you decide to settle down.'

'Thanks Joe,' was Tom's reply.

'Jesus, Tom, nobody could be more delighted for you than me, except Ma, I suppose, but if I was you I'd shove that aside until this business is done. From what you say, this is only starting to get stirred.' Joe gave his advice gently, his arm around his brother's shoulders.

'For an eejit, you make an awful lot of sense,' Tom conceded.

Their conversation turned to the business Tom had been forced to neglect. Joe filled him in on the progress of their animals – the training of the two mares, the increased demand for their services, created by the goodwill invested in their business by Tom's actions. They had to hire a man permanently to handle the fuel end, while Joe took care of deliveries and removals, grabbing every free moment to pursue the training of the mares.

'Be glad when you get your arse back to work,' Joe said joking.

'Won't be too long now,' Tom promised, adding, 'with a bit of luck.'

Chapter 28

That Saturday evening Tom had dinner with his parents. It was an enjoyable evening for everyone except Rose. Tom, with an end in sight, Martin diabolically delighted with his son's progress, Joe bovinely serene. Rose alone was apprehensive. She maintained the mother's prerogative – worry for her family, her son's safety. Unable to share in the jubilation, and unwilling to dampen their spirits, she served the meal and excused herself. The men drank and laughed. Martin sang and expressed his pride in his warrior son.

'You have the son-of-a-bitch on the run,' he bragged. 'He'll have to come out to play. You're making him look like a gobshite.'

Joe interrupted, saying, 'Da, this is not kids stuff. There's big money being lost here. He can afford to sit back and get the people working for him to deal with hassles like Tom.'

'How could he keep his respect if he let someone else do his job for him?' Martin demanded.

'It doesn't matter who does the job, Da, he gets respect because the job gets done. The power to get it done – that's what gets respect,' Tom told him.

'Tom's biggest chance is that at the moment he's in the public eye. Too many people are watching every move he makes. He's too hard to get at quietly. That's his protection right now. When this dies down, that's the time he'll have to start worrying,' was Joe's tuppence worth.

'The divil take it! Martin cursed. 'Has the man no balls at all?'

'Balls have nothing to do with it. We're hurting their business. What they do about it will be a business decision,' Tom explained.

Martin wanted nothing to do with this logic, but continued to ramble on about manhood and shame and being worth your salt. His sons smiled and tried to calculate how much he'd had to drink before dinner.

'Break his black fucking heart!' Martin said.

Sunday and Monday Tom maintained the pretence of waiting for dealers. His cheerful expectancy made his companions forget their impatience. The unrewarded days of waiting passed easily. Tuesday morning dawned. Tom was awake at the first light. He drank cup after cup of tea and considered his responsibility on the coming day. Repeatedly the people had been told that the dealers must surely produce weapons the next time they came. It had been emphasised again and again that they should have no qualms, indeed must back off, at the first hint of such an occurrence. This would be simply a strategic retreat on their part. Afterwards they would meet and plan their answer to such a contingency. Tom worried at the prospect of people ignoring this order. How to enforce this order, protect his friends at all costs: His action alone had led to their being involved to the extent that they were at present. He hoped, as before, they would accept his command. If not, he could do nothing else but play it by ear.

Chapter 29

Before the rest of the house awakened Tom went outside and fed and watered his mare. Satisfied she had taken enough, he took a brush and groomed her shaggy coat. She would look her best today, possibly her last day of battle. He hoped that after today her activities would be confined to pulling a cart. He was standing back admiring his handiwork when Joe's voice sounded softly behind him.

'Special day?' Joe's intuitive question.

'Yes,' Tom admitted. He went on to explain at last his inside knowledge, his arrangement with the guards.

'Good,' Joe said, 'I was wondering how ye could come back against guns. I wonder how many more were thinking on those lines?'

'I'd say quite a few, but it seemed sensible to keep the arrangement secret. If there are no heroes today nobody will get hurt among our own. The guards and the lads are pros. They'll play it as they see fit. Just so long as we're out of the way fast. Keep your fingers crossed, brother,' was Tom's prayerful reply.

'I think I'll take the day off today,' Joe said. 'I imagine I might be useful around the Tosh.'

'Good idea,' Tom agreed. 'See that everyone scarpers at the first sign of a gun. I just wish there was some way to let them know all over the city, but there's no way that the word wouldn't get to the dealers. Let's hope the guards have been as cute.'

Rose called them in to breakfast. Martin was shovelling rashers and eggs and doorsteps of bread into himself, washing it down with a small bucket of sweet tea.

'There's a mare out back that hasn't got the constitution you have Da,' Joe joked to his father.

'She's young yet,' he answered full-mouthed.

Rose watched Tom, her mother's intuition knowing this was the day. Tom's only means of reassuring her was a devil-may-care wink. It didn't seem to work. Martin left. The man had his own career to pursue. Joe discreetly left.

'Troubled, Ma?' Tom asked.

'I'm worried for you, Tom,' she admitted.

He explained to his mother what he anticipated that day. 'I wish it were as simple as just worrying about me,' Tom said gravely. 'I'm more worried about the other people involved. I'm in this on account of a horse. They're in it for their families. When the time comes to retreat they may be more afraid to lose this chance to clean up their streets than scared at the possibility of getting hurt.'

'Tom, son,' Rose insisted, 'don't make little of your own reason. It might have been the reason to start with, but you're just as much concerned as they are about making the streets safe for the kids, for Tommy.'

A knock at the front door ended their conversation. A teenage boy stood on the step. 'Billy told me to tell you they'll be ready in twenty minutes at the library, Mr. Reid,' he recited his message.

Tom nodded his understanding, and seeing the boy's bright eagerness said, 'The mare is ready out the back, if you'd like to lead her out.'

The boy shot round to the back and Tom entered the house again. He donned his denim jacket. His mother approached almost shyly. He met her and embraced her tightly.

'Don't worry, Ma,' he reassured her gently, 'I'll send someone to let you know as soon as it's over.'

The boy stood proudly holding the reins of the huge mare on the footpath. Tom emerged from the house, the hurley stick under his arm, lighting a cigarette.

'What's your name, son?' Tom asked him.

'Ben — short for Bernard,' the boy told him shyly.

'Okay, Ben, why don't you lead the mare, while I finish this fag,' Tom said, earning the boy's lifetime gratitude and admiration. 'And, please leave off the mister, my name is Tom.'

The boy nodded, flushed, unable to divert his attention for one second from the responsibility of the mare, and unable to conceal his pleasure at the envious stares of the other youngsters as they passed. In the relative privacy of the first lane, the words eventually spilled from the boy's lips. By the time the pair reached the Library, Tom knew the boy's family as well as he knew his own.

Tom met Billy's outstretched hand warmly with his own, a firm friendship developing between the two men. Billy informed him of their preparations and waited for any suggestions Tom might have wanted to make. Leaving the mare in the boy's eager care, Tom led Billy aside. He detailed his meeting with the superintendent, explaining his silence thus far. Billy thought for a moment, his features drawn before speaking.

'Jaysus, Tom, what are you playing at?' he paused. 'The fucking law. They don't give two shits for our problems.' Billy shook his head disgustedly as he continued. 'We could have handled it ourselves.'

'How, Billy? By tooling up the men, women and children. We're talking about guns. Cops get paid to face guns. They're armed and they're supposed to be trained.' Tom spoke with a measured contempt. 'Besides, they're going to get involved anyway. Let it be when it's to our advantage, not theirs. Let them have the glory, we need the results.'

Billy nodded, as if some invisible hand was forcing the movement. 'I know you're right Tom, but I just hate the idea.'

'So do I Billy, and if my past couple of years doesn't tell you that, fuck it.' Tom shrugged the matter aside and continued. 'Joe knows. I told him this morning. He's sticking by the Tosh, so there should be no nasty surprises there. Us knowing this will keep any would-be heroes from getting themselves killed.'

The conversation was halted there by the arrival of a shouting teenage boy. A lone dealer was strolling down a street, sort of half-way between the areas covered by Tom and the Tosh. Billy's eyes found Tom's. Quickly he proferred, 'Diversion?' Tom nodded.

Billy spoke urgently to a man beside him. The man with an exaggerated wink acknowledged Billy's words and moved with crab-like rapidity through the surrounding people. He entered a waiting car. Immediately it sped off down the scheme. At the same time Tom was painstakingly imparting the message he wanted passed down the line. His listeners understood his strategy as he urged them importantly to their task. Even as they were leaving, Billy was telling him, 'I put the Tosh wide – only cars.'

Tom didn't acknowledge. He knew Billy by now. Instead, he said ominously, 'It's going to happen very soon.'

Both men swiftly rolled cigarettes, lit them, and seemed to withdraw momentarily from the surroundings. Around them a quiet settled. The big piebald mare whinnied. As she began, Tom was already moving. Gently he removed the reins from the hands of the patient boy. The hand with the reins was gripping the hemplike mane and the rider vaulted easily onto the broad back. His eye caught the waving motion of a distant arm off to his left. Thighs and heels spurred the heavy animal forward. Half-way to that waving figure, a young voice shouted to the passing Tom, 'A big Fiat, blue!' and louder as the horseman moved away, 'The Parade, four guys.'

The shouting youth watched, stunned for a few seconds, then excitement took him and he shot off after the big mare.

Chapter 30

Reaching the end of the lane that joined the Parade, the boy slowed and saw the mounted figure approach the big car.

Tom, from his vantage point atop the mare, quickly appraised the scene before him. The blue Fiat at the kerb to his right facing him. A figure walking away from the car towards a nearby house. Fifty or sixty people at the opposite side of the road, and more on the road behind the car, all keeping a distance, awaiting his arrival. Further on, at the point where the Parade ended, he could see the heavy barrels being rolled into place, blocking the road. Behind him, he knew, concrete pillars already blocked that end of the street. Slowly, he inched the mare towards the car. On his left, he glimpsed Billy herding the people, his urgent whispers communicating perfectly the advisability of their moving quietly towards the rear of the car.

In the car the driver was telling the men in the back to watch the crowd. He'd take care of the Apache. As the crowd passed behind his line of vision he reached between the seats and lifted a sawn-off shotgun. He rested the short barrel on the support of his side mirror, at the same time surveying the retreating crowd in that same mirror. He concentrated on the horse and rider before him. To himself he silently said, 'So this is the hardchaw who started all the hassle that has me here in a car in the morning with a fucking shotgun in my hands.' Aloud he informed Tom, 'You're getting into the range of this thing.'

The calm of the horseman's reply unnerved him. 'I know.'

The rider had stopped. The moment he heard the 'Jesus,' from the back seat of the car, he knew. A quick look in the mirror told him the people had disappeared, and in their place, emerging from between the houses all around them, were men with guns, holding them in a way that immediately communicated their familiarity with those weapons. They were surrounded. 'Shit!' was his philosophical comment. To his mates in the car he said, 'Do exactly as they say. These fuckers would just love to blow us to bits.'

As instructed, their weapons were tossed from the car and the four men got out awkwardly, their hands flat upon their heads. In seconds their arms were hand-cuffed behind their backs and bags of evidence were being produced gingerly from the car.

A tall, young detective approached Tom. He carried a walkie-talkie radio.

'We've nicked another car-load down the scheme where the other guy on the horse was,' he informed Tom, and added with a smile, 'Nobody hurt.'

Tom thanked him. The detective saluted him jokingly with the radio and walked away.

The barrels had been pulled off the road and the police vehicles were piling in. Each one of the four prisoners was given the luxury of a personal car and the company of three policemen. One of the arriving cars disgorged the Superintendent. He spoke curtly to several of the detectives, making his way towards the mounted Tom. He stopped at the mare's head, and stroking her absentmindedly, demonstrating a familiarity with horses, said conversationally, 'My father was the last in his area to use the horse on the farm. The plough and the mower and a lot more stuff are still on the old place. He was a man of imagination, but I bet he never considered the use you've been putting the mare to. She's a fine animal, looks well cared for.' He paused, looking up at Tom, allowing time for him to comment. Tom didn't.

'Your stallion must be a fine animal,' he continued.

'He is.' Tom replied, meeting the policeman's speculative gaze coldly.

'Anyway, it's becoming a very successful day all round.' The Super changed the subject with the ease of one used to being listened to. 'Two car-loads of villains here, with the evidence to convict. Reports are starting to filter in from the other areas. It seems the lads are tripping over themselves to be apprehended. Oh yes, a very successful day.'

Tom laughed. 'A very successful day like this won't do your career any harm either.'

The Superintendent joined Tom in laughter. Tom noted his laughter was real, expressing an unashamedly pleasurable satisfaction.

'Very true, Mr. Reid, very true,' he chuckled. Still laughing, the policeman acknowledged, 'Why, thank you, Tom, thank you indeed.'

He beckoned to a passing uniformed guard and spoke some words to him. The guard went to the car in which the Super had arrived. Her returned with two apples for his superior. The Super fed one to the mare. The other he tossed up to Tom who caught it instinctively.

'I'll be seeing you,' he promised, turning to leave.

Behind him Tom was munching the apple.

Chapter 31

The reporter was excited: 'Extraordinary – 27 cars confiscated, 62 villains nicked, 51 guns and a kilo of smack.'

Billy reckoned it was far more important that the people now knew they could hold their streets.

Surrounded by admirers the Tosh was re-living that last adrenalin-pumping ride to face the gun.

Joe was at the bar getting two pints, admiring the knees of a redheaded lady, reminding himself of a potential order for a ton of logs, noting Tom nodding in agreement with a guy he had absolutely no time for.

The County Bar was playing host to a clientele of winners.

Two pints in hand, elbows as efficient as electric prods, Joe detached Tom and herded him to a quiet corner.

'Sláinte!' Joe toasted his brother.

Tom smiled half-heartedly.

'Some day, huh?' Joe probed.

'Couldn't have been better,' Tom admitted.

'Everyone else is celebrating Tom?'

'For everyone else something is settled. They've won themselves a future. They have made their streets safer for their kids,' Tom paused. 'Me, I'm still chasing a stallion. Am I any closer?'

Joe draped his arm around his brother's shoulders, leaned close and spoke quietly. 'You set out to thwart the Cur's business here in Ballyer, right? Dammit, you closed him down. You set out to embarrass him with the Board. Shit, Tom, you damn near closed them down. The way I read that, your life probably isn't worth tuppence right now, but that doesn't seem to worry you a bit.'

Tom didn't think that was a question, so Joe continued.

'Listen, my son, you've done a hell of a lot more than even *you* expected, certainly more than I did. Tom, it's their move. Relax for a while, get footless today because tomorrow you're going to be watching your arse.'

Two pints were placed on the table before them.

'One more thing, Tom. Don't be missing Marie and the boy. They're where they have to be now. Your concern is here. You'll have them when it's over. You won't have them before.'

'That's a great combination,' Tom mused, 'the red hair and the green eyes.'

'Who are you telling?' Joe said, as he walked away.

Tom woke up before his hangover the next morning, sneaked into the kitchen and had a poitín punch and a good breakfast before it caught up with him. The hangover left in disgust.

He began a normal day. As normal a day as any day that might be your last. Joe's words and the wild party he was thereafter able to enjoy had set him straight. He had a time of waiting and watching to pass, and what better way to pass it than the way he liked. His first job was the two mares in the back. He fed and watered them, with scraps from the kitchen they liked so much. Watching them, he drank another mug of strong tea and smoked a meditative cigarette. He then led them to the meagre grazing across the road, accepted the offer 'to mind' them from an early-rising boy and returned to the pile of logs. It didn't look any smaller than the last time he'd taken an axe to it. Joe had not come home yet, so he didn't know what was on that day. He started chopping logs. Within minutes he was sweating, lost in the simple pleasure of pure physical labour. Joe returned later and briefed him on the business of the following week. Thus, for the rest of that week Tom returned to the life he loved, a life whose every action related in some way to the horses he loved so much. This life, however, was now governed by a constant vigilance and suppressed expectation. Tom held his excitement at bay with hard work and patience.

Unnoticed by Tom, his every move was watched. Not by those he had to fear, but by the people who sought, in gratitude, to see no harm came to him. During that week the Committee had solidified its network. Sensibly, not resting on the dramatic laurels of their successful campaign, they realised that community awareness was the key to safe and healthy neighbourhoods. With such an intelligence network in operation it was a simple matter to keep an eye out for the man who had provided the inspiration for their disciplined vigilance.

That high summer week rolled into the week-end. The first week-end of a new month. For the brothers it was an important date. Every first Sunday of the month hailed the Smithfield Horse Fair. A large cobbled square on the north side of the Liffey, Smithfield was the site every morning of the fruit and vegetable markets. On the first Sunday of the month it was taken over by the horsemen of the city as a venue, a showplace for their animals. Here everything to do with horses and ponies could be bought and sold. This was the stock exchange of the equine community. Here was the place where current values were set on the livestock of the city. No owner or breeder worth his salt could afford to miss this event, if not to buy or sell, then just for a glimpse at the state of the market, or to catch up with the gossip.

While Tom had been preoccupied with heroics, Joe, with the help of the Jobber, had completed the training of the two mares. Two strong mares, trained to the shafts, were valuable enough to provide the brothers with working cash, or with at least twice that number of new animals to train.

They decided to bring them to market. On the Saturday they brought one of their own working mares to the Jobber's and returned with the two young mares to the house. Sunday morning they drove one of their carts towards town, the two animals tethered behind. On the cart with them were the Jobber, and their father, Martin. A fair day was something neither countryman could resist. It was a gorgeous, sunny morning, as they entered the excitement of the cobbled square. Tom's recent adventures made him the sought-after man at the market. With Tom thus occupied, Joe took care of the business of trading, a business at which he excelled. By twelve he'd disposed of the mares and had already acquired three fine young animals. Tom was in the centre of a group of congratulatory horsemen when he felt a tugging at his sleeve.

'Mister, are you Tonto Reid?' a young boy of about eight

was asking him.

'That's who I am, son,' Tom told him.

'A little man in that pub over there gave me a pound to tell you he'd like to see you when you have a chance.' The boy recited his message breathlessly.

Tom smiled his understanding to the boy. He produced a pound from his pocket and said, 'You go back over there and tell the little man that Tom Reid gave you a pound to tell him "He'll be over in a few minutes and that he should have a pint ready for him." Have you got that?'

The youngster repeated the message, and clutching his second pound rushed back to the pub. Joe, who had been watching this exchange, gave Tom an enquiring look.

'The Wren,' Tom reckoned.

They both knew without speaking that this was probably what they'd been waiting for all week. Tom excused himself to the men he'd been talking with and strolled through the crowds towards the pub.

Joe hailed Martin, who was arguing with another old man in the vicinity and bade him urgently to take charge of the animals. He followed quickly in Tom's footsteps.

On entering the pub he scanned the dim interior. He soon spotted Tom shaking hands with the Wren and seating himself beside him. He checked the rest of the crowded bar but saw nothing to arouse his suspicion. He took a stool at the bar and ordered a drink, carefully observing the room. The Wren saw him and smiled over reassuringly. It seemed there was nothing to worry about, but anyway . . .

'Howya, Tom?' was the Wren's greeting as they shook hands.

'Benny!' was Tom's friendly reply.

Unhurriedly they passed the pleasantries of friends meeting. After a time, having disposed of queries about family and friends, they ordered another round and savoured, silently awhile, the good Guinness.

The Wren eventually spoke. 'Well, Tommy boy, you've gone and done it,' he began, laughing. 'You really fucked them up. The only one contending in the unpopularity stakes against you is my illustrious boss. Between the two of you you've cost the Board about a quarter of their business. I wonder if you have any idea how much that's worth. At the going rate of having a man killed, yourself and himself are dead a thousand times over. Pissed off as the Board is about the loss of business, that's nothing compared with their being pissed off at the loss of face.'

The Wren paused, looking at the silent Tom. He continued. 'Everyone knows the Board exists, but very few know who they are. Now every villain and his cousin who works in the Corporation knows who one of them is. Tommy, boy, that Board does not like you. But as I already mentioned, they like the Cur even less.'

'Now isn't that nice?' Tom interrupted.

'You keep listening, my son. I'm only getting to the good bit.' Benny told him. 'The Board seems to have given this a few days' thought, without the benefit of the Cur's presence. Then on Friday they issued him with an invitation to attend an exclusive meeting. I wasn't invited, but then I never am. I was waiting for himself in the bar of the Burlington. We usually have a drink after the meetings, but this time he appears like a demon and drags me immediately out to the car. He's fucking fuming. Takes me about an hour and him a gram or two of coke before he tells me the score.'

Getting two more pints gave them pause and allowed Tom to consider what he'd heard so far. The Wren continued: 'It seems the Board made him a little proposition. Seeing as the little wrinkle was his doing, their words, they felt that the solution should be in his hands. The business could be rebuilt or made up in another area, but the loss of face was another story. That would have to be sorted out immediately. This little wrinkle could be solved very simply. The Cur was told he would have to kill you, personally. They emphasised *personally*, because knowing the Cur as they do, he'd as soon hire somebody else to do it. No, the only way for him to prove his worth and demonstrate that he meant business, was for him to waste you, personally.'

The little man paused now, to allow this to sink in. He watched Tom swallow the information. Getting no response, he went on.

'An ingenious little solution, I have to admit,' he commented. 'The way I see it, the Cur is dead as far as they are concerned. His days are numbered. They know he's fucked up with the coke. If he kills you, fine, but if you kill him, I think that would suit them better. There's a good chance you'd get nicked for it and you know nothing that could compromise them. There's their problem solved, right there. If he kills you, then they have to waste him. But then maybe your brother, or one of your friends might do that for them. Anyway, they just sit for a while and see what happens.'

Again he stopped. Tom being still silent, he continued. 'And as I see it, if you sort him out and I mean *kill* him, I reckon they'll leave you alone. Do you see that, Tom?'

'Yeah,' Tom said hoarsely, 'I see that.'

'Okay then,' Benny said, and put his hand on Tom's shoulder. 'What I've told you so far I would have told you anyway as a friend. In fact I have told you that as a friend. What I tell you now, I tell you as the Cur's messenger boy. He says if you want your stallion he'll be in the Backers tomorrow morning at ten with your horse and if you're not there he'll kill it. And you and I both know he will.'

Tom remained silent, impassive. The Wren went to the bar where he ordered two pints and waited while they were being pulled. He spoke quietly with Joe as he waited. Minutes later he returned to the table. He looked down at Tom, deep in thought, and sat.

'You alright?' Tom reassured him.

'I have the car round the corner,' the Wren told him. 'In the boot there's a shooter. Do you want it?'

'No, Benny,' was Tom's unhesitating reply.

'You know the Cur is going to be carrying?'

'Of course,' Tom said. 'It's not heroics on my part, Benny. As you say, if I kill him, the Board will probably leave me be. But the law is a different matter. If I meet him with a gun there's grounds for premeditation. I've got to find another way. I don't want to spend anymore time away from my kid.'

'I hope you can find another way, Tommy, though I don't know why I'm encouraging you. I'm only creating my own redundancy,' Benny joked.

'Go away, Benny, you've probably been robbing the bastard blind. I'd say you have the price of a pub,' Tom smiled.

'This is the way you want it to go, isn't it?' the Wren lapsed back into seriousness.

'Exactly, Benny. Exactly.' Tom admitted.

He waved Joe over to the table and the three friends began to talk easily about the things friends talk about on a pleasant Sunday morning in summer.

Chapter 32

'I don't know what to say to Ma,' Tom was saying to his father.

They sat with their legs over the side of the slowly-moving cart on their way back to Ballyer. He'd told his father exactly what had transpired with the Wren that morning.

'Say nothing,' was Martin's advice. 'You'll only have her fretting for nothing. I know you're going to settle that black bastard once and for all. Least said, soonest mended.'

'Jesus, Da, she'll guess there's something wrong. She always does,' Tom confessed.

'Then you'd better be a great actor today. That's all there is for it,' his father told him.

The three mares tied behind the cart were skittish with the newness of their surroundings. Tom calmed them and looked at the smiling countenance of his father. Joe, the Jobber, sat chatting on the pile of sacks that passed for a seat at the front of the cart.

'What the fuck are you so happy about?' Tom asked his father.

'Our plan worked perfectly,' he beamed.

'You're a crazy old fart!' Tom laughed. 'Our plan? What's this *our*. Besides, tomorrow I could be like a collander. Our plan!'

He finished pretending exasperation.

'Yes,' the old man said righteously, 'our plan. Who put the idea in your head in the first place. While you were farting around?'

'You don't give two fucks if I get killed or not!' Tom upbraided his father.

'If you can't handle a rat like that, then you're not the son I reared.' Martin spat back. 'Maybe you'd like your daddy to take care of it for you?'

Tom raised his eyes to heaven and prayed aloud, 'Protect me from my friends, and especially my sainted father.'

Martin ignored the gibe: 'Don't forget, nothing to your mother.'

Tom turned to calm the three animals following.

Over the Sunday dinner Tom followed his father's advice and acted as he'd never acted before. Gratefully, he saw his mother suspected nothing of the enormity of his burden. After dinner Tom spent an hour in the shed at the back of the house. How to take the Cur! In his mind he saw the Backers, one of the playgrounds of his childhood. How often had they played cowboys, war? How many ambushes had he enacted in that playground? He tried to remember, had the Cur been part of these games? Probably, but Tom was sure that it was a long time since the Cur had engaged in such fantasies, whereas he had spent many happy hours with young Tommy, leading the boy through the pleasures of his own youth. Pleasures he had seen the kids nowadays rejecting, their imaginations shrinking under the onslaught of TV, everything laid out for them on that little screen. Tom knew instinctively the benefits of play, the necessity of play. Jesus, he thought to himself, what have I been doing for the last few weeks only playing cowboys. The value of play. Now I'll play again, 'for real' as they used to say.

He took a walk down the scheme to the house of the man known as the Pickeroony, a man whose magpie tendency provided him with a hobby that paid, a scrap collector and a hoarder. His house was actually smaller than Tom's, lacking a side entrance, and positioned in the middle of a block of six. Outside, half on the road, half on the pavement, stood the battered cart he used for his foraging expeditions. The mare he used to pull the cart Tom knew would be somewhere nearby in whatever piece of free grazing the Pick had tethered it until it was discovered and a complaining householder would come and force him to move it. A solitary man, his grimy lifestyle precluded him from the orderly pleasure of wife and family. Front and back garden were piled high with the debris of the consumer society.

Every room in the house was a library of nuts and bolts, electric motors, lawnmower blades, a thousand pieces of dismantled engineering. The Pickeroony sat on an upturned fridge in the front garden, screwdriver in hand, a hand in which every line was etched clearly with thirty years of eager groping in the bowels of oil-blackened machinery. Tom noted that on those hands were none of the cuts or sores expected on the hands of one working with sharp edges and slipping spanners. Engrained they might be, but the sureness and precision of his movements, the delicacy of his touch, his instinctive understanding of the exact amount of force required for any task, made those hands the cobwebbed hands of a piano player. He was also a man who wasted no energy on words.

'Tom.' He greeted.

'Half-inch ball-bearings,' Tom's respectful reply.

'How many?'

'Couple o' dozen.'

The Pick entered the house and emerged minutes later with the required items in a brown paper bag. Tom checked the contents and asked, 'What do I owe you?'

'Two bags of logs.'

'I'll drop them down during the week,' Tom assured him.

'No hurry.' The Pick closed the conversation by taking up the screwdriver and returning his attention to the task he had to abandon in order to deal with the inconvenience of business.

Marie's house was Tom's next stop. He let himself in, went immediately to Tommy's room. He found what he was looking for, the hunting sling he'd bought for the boy some time previously. He checked the heavy-duty rubber, and finding it slightly frayed removed and replaced it with the spare he'd bought with the original purchase. A dangerous little weapon, like any 'gat' he'd made for himself as a boy. Different only in the addition of an arm-piece which made for greater leverage. He'd spent several days with young Tommy, making sure the boy fully understood the responsibility of owning such a potentially dangerous weapon.

He packed the sling and the ball-bearings into a duffle bag of the boy's and left the house. Back at his mother's, he made sure she wasn't home before retiring to the back shed. Joe kept an old machete there he used for chopping kindling. Tom took it to the bench and began to put a razor edge on it. Sharpened, he put it into the bag and hid the bag under the bench. He was armed now for the coming fight. To avoid confronting his mother, Tom chose absence as discretion, and left the house.

He frequented pubs that night, not ordinarily used, and passed the solitary time thinking. Not the serious thoughts of anticipation, rather the luxury of memories and a little fantasy about the future. He was sensible enough to know that until after the following day he could not afford anything more than to imagine whimsically the possibility of a future. Towards the end of the evening, however, he fell into conversation with an old man and spent a pleasant hour listening to tales of times past.

Walking home, he allowed himself to think of the following day, the day he realised he'd been working for in the previous weeks. Tomorrow, he would get to the Backers several hours before the time the Cur nominated, survey the field, climb into the Cur's head and be ready. There was no more he could do now other than get a good night's sleep. That's what he did. He arose at five and fed himself toast, fried eggs and tea. As he collected the bag from the shed Joe appeared at his side.

'You're going?' he asked.

Tom nodded.

'You have everything you need?' He was eyeing the bag.

'If I can anticipate his thinking a little, then I'll have everything I need,' he assured Joe.

'Anything I can do?' Joe said with unaccustomed emotion.

'There is, Joe.' Tom said. 'Take care of business till I get back.'

The brothers embraced quickly and furiously, and Tom walked away.

Joe's words hung in the morning air behind him: 'Good luck.'

Tom took the shortest route to the Backers, entering the area from the back of Oranmore Road. He patrolled the shrinking fields of the Backers for an hour-and-a-half until he had a clear picture burned in behind his eyes. Originally farmed fields, now with disuse the hedgerows had swollen and spread, creating small clear spaces surrounded by close entanglements of stunted trees and thornbushes. Tom reviewed his previous knowledge of the access points between the spaces, checking the inevitable overgrowth on these same passages and the creation of new openings. When he was satisfied he moved towards the only bridge that spanned the narrow valley of the railway into the Backers. If the Cur was indeed bringing the stallion, as he had said, then it was reasonable to expect he would cross that bridge.

There was no way he'd ride that stallion far, if indeed he'd ride it at all. He would use a trailer. He'd get as close as possible before hampering himself with controlling a big, nervous animal. He could drive right to that bridge and be in the Backers within seconds. Tom reckoned a coke-sniffer, living in Foxrock, luxuriating in the good life, would not relish leading a spirited stallion through the labyrinth of bushes he would certainly not be familiar with. No. He'd come in the easy way and use the horse to flush Tom out.

Tom climbed a tree, the height of which gave him sight of most of the surrounding ground. The full summer growth of the tree hid him from detection. Once quietly settled, the many birds around him resumed their morning song. It was just gone eight. The Cur might decide to come early. Tom rolled a half-dozen cigarettes, put five in an accessible pocket, lit the sixth and relaxed. All he could do now was wait. For Tom the time simply passed. Comfortable in the tree, he lost himself in the birdsong. The birds were his eyes and ears. Like a miner in a tunnel, the canary is the alarm. When song stops there's something wrong. The approaching car alerted Tom and the birds simultaneously. The birds identified the danger as none of theirs and resumed their song. Tom extinguished his cigarette, watching the bridge. The blue Mercedes and the trailer approached, turned slowly and reversed across, stopping on Tom's side of the bridge. The Cur emerged. A tall man in Berber jacket and denim trousers, horsey clothes. He stepped around to the trailer. Tom saw the disgruntlement in his walk. He might have the clothes, he did not have the core of fishing, shooting and riding. He walked like he was avoiding dogshit.

Tom knew his stallion. He was not easy to handle. The Cur dealt with him easily, if a little angrily. This meant power and aggression. He might be scattered, but he was fit and well coordinated. He led the stallion with his left hand and removed a pistol from the pocket of his jacket with the right.

From above, Tom saw the path he'd figured he'd take. He saw the space the man and horse neared, and anticipated this as the Cur's first possible stand. A rough circle of coarse grass surrounded by tangled hedgerows. From above, laid out for him like a map, Tom memorised the network of passages that honeycombed the bushes, all invisible to a man standing in the clearing. He slid from the tree and chose his position, near the forefront of the undergrowth. Plenty of cover, standing sparse enough to shoot through, crouched, he withdrew the ballbearings from the bag and put them in the right-hand pocket of his short jacket. Leaving the sling aside, he rolled the bag tightly around the machete, a makeshift scabbard, and slid it under his belt on the left-hand side. He picked up the sling and fit a bearing into the tongue, and held it loosely, ready for firing. He waited. For a moment Tom had the uncanny feeling the Cur knew exactly where he was. He quickly shrugged off this foolishness.

'Reid'?' the Cur screamed. 'Show yourself, or I'll cripple the horse.'

Tom remained silent. He aimed the sling at the spot he expected the Cur's head to appear and waited.

'Come out, Reid. You know I'm not bluffing!' Again the hoarse threat.

Tom decided to bluff instead. The sling aimed head-high just under the neck of the stallion. 'Go ahead,' he invited.

The Cur looked around the front of the big animal, seeking the source of the voice. His left eye exploded in a red agony as the ballbearing struck home. A second missile struck the flanks of the already nervous stallion. He reared, tearing the reins from the Cur's hand and bounded away. Terrified now, the stallion circled the clearing like a circus animal in the ring. He was too frightened to see the gaps that would release him from the clearing. Tom was already far away from the spot he'd shot from, in position and watching the convulsions of the Cur. He had a handkerchief pressed to his bleeding eye. His scream was now of pain, coupled with his previous anger. Tom took a chance. He watched the circuit of the stallion, breaking cover just as it reached him. Grasping the mane as it passed, he threw himself on the back of the charging animal and kneed him through the nearest gap. Two bullets whizzed past him before he gained the cover of the next field. He crossed two more clearings before he slowed the stallion.

Dismounting, he calmed the excited animal. Slowly the birds resumed their song. If the Cur followed he would know. Here he would betray himself. Tom weighed up his position. Could he just ride away? The Cur a survivor? His empire depended on killing Tom. That was the sunset he had to ride into. He was not giving up either one.

The dealer's clumsiness in this environment was Tom's only advantage. Why wait for the street, there he had cars, hirelings, power. Tom reckoned he was about half a mile from the Jobber's farm. Too far to ride there, get back and still retain his edge on the Cur. Trusting the stallion's memory of the comfort of his own home paddock, he removed the bridle and slapped its chestnut rump. 'Go on,' he urged. The stallion covered less than ten yards when he slowed, uncertain. Tom roared this time, 'Go on!'

As the stallion took off, so did Tom. His shout had cost him his invisibility. He circled back, bent low, using the cover. He stopped when he estimated he was half-way from where he'd last seen the Cur, as close to the open ground as he dared. He sat peering through the bush. It was too quiet. The Cur was near.

Tom saw the arm with the gun first. It was a Luger. The left eye in the face was closed and bloody. Outrage and pain made the big man clumsier than ever. Tom let him pass. His next ball-bearing struck soundly the back of his opponent's head. Screaming, the Cur spun and fired blindly behind him. Tom was already moving to get behind him. The ball-bearings at that range packed a hell of a punch. The pain was followed by nausea. Shaking the head only emphasised both. The Cur's hot anger turned cold. He finally realised he was as much hunted as he was the hunter. Thirty feet away Tom watched him breathe deeply several times, then scan the bush. Tom struck him three more times, ineffectual hits, designed solely to disconcert. After each one the bullets reached closer to him. After the second shot, the Cur reloaded with an efficiency that startled Tom. After the third, Tom moved ahead and crawled from the cover of the bushes and lay flat among thigh-high nettles. He withdrew the machete, ignoring the stings to his face and curled up, minimising himself. A snake-in-the-grass, he smiled at his own foolishness, the gamble he had to take. One-eyed, he hoped the Cur would get close enough, feel secure enough away from the bushes, to keep coming.

'Dermot,' Tom whispered derisively, barely loud enough.

Bullets flew, inches above him, into the bushes. Then the arm with the gun was above him, the Cur's attention on the cover. Tom came up fast, shoulder under the gun-arm. With both hands he drove the machete up into the pit of the Cur's stomach. The force of his drive knocked the Cur backwards. Tom on top of him, an obscene embrace that pushed the blade through into the ground beneath. The handle was hurting Tom's stomach, but he did not take his weight off it until he had shaken the gun from the dying man's hand. He stood up and kicked the gun aside. He wanted no fingerprints on it but the Cur's. His hands, when he looked at them surprised him by having no blood on them. The Cur stared silently up at him, his dying face strangely expressionless, bland as a baby in a pram. Tom walked away in the direction of the Jobber's.

The stallion was looking splendid, groomed and frisky, back in the loving care of the Jobber. He pranced around the paddock he'd been away from for so long.

'It's as it was,' the Jobber gleamed. 'There's tea on the stove.'

In the dusty calm of the cottage Tom sipped the strong tea. The dogs snored, the cat in the heat of the window licked a shine onto its black flanks. Outside, the birds sang and the stallion mounted the new mare.

Chapter 33

Tom sat in the Super's room at the station. Foote was behind the desk. A young detective entered, looking at the senior officer, uncertain if he should report with Tom in the room.

'Speak man!' Foote said, impatiently.

'It's as he said, sir,' the detective began. 'McMurragh is nailed to the ground with a goddamned machete, a Luger beside him. We sent that to the lab for fingerprints. The victim is fairly battered around the head, eye closed and swollen, cheek split, back of the head split. None of those injuries look serious enough to have killed him. Jesus!' he added incredulously. 'A sling?'

Foote waved him out.

'Why did you come in?' he asked Tom. He did not wait for an answer. He continued, 'You'd have been our prime suspect, but certainly not our only one. That bastard was not the most popular man in Dublin. Proving you did it might have been difficult.'

Tom rolled a cigarette before he replied.

'I want this finished.' Tom said. 'I don't think you like unsolved cases. You might think that was untidy.' He looked down at the Superintendent's handmade shoes. 'If you stepped in shit you wouldn't throw those away. You, or one of your lads, more likely, would keep at them until they were spotless.'

The policeman's laugh annoyed Tom, but somehow it reminded him of Joe's. Where Joe's was sure and heartfelt, Foote's was smug with position and power, but sure. Tom wondered would he ever feel that sure. Then he thought of Marie and Tommy, and the stallion back with the herd, his life reassembled as he wanted it. He himself would always have to walk the tightrope, carrying his past like the long pole, for balance.

The policeman interrupted his thoughts. 'The investigation may take a while. Justice moves slowly. I see no reason to lock you up for the moment, but don't leave the country.'

He turned his attention to some papers on the desk. Tom took this as a signal that he was dismissed. He rose, and opened the door. As he was stepping outside, he heard the Superintendent's parting words: 'Au Revoir.'